Two of a Kind

Other *Avon Camelot Books* by
Ann Gabhart

DISCOVERY AT COYOTE POINT

Avon Flare Books

WISH COME TRUE

ANN GABHART is the author of more than a dozen books for young people including *Discovery at Coyote Point* which is also available from Avon Camelot Books. She lives in Lawrenceburg, Kentucky.

Two of a Kind

ANN GABHART

AN AVON  CAMELOT BOOK

TWO OF A KIND is an original publication of Avon Books. This work has
never before appeared in book form.

AVON BOOKS
A division of
The Hearst Corporation
1350 Avenue of the Americas
New York, New York 10019

First Avon Camelot Printing: March 1992

CAMELOT TRADEMARK REG. U.S. PAT. OFF. AND IN OTHER COUNTRIES. MARCA
REGISTRADA. HECHO EN U.S.A.

Printed in the U.S.A.

OPM 10 9 8 7 6 5 4 3 2 1

Chapter 1

"It won't last," Birdie Honaker whispered to herself when she spotted her aunt waiting for her at the airport. "It won't last."

Birdie edged over behind two men in dark suits who were exchanging business cards as they walked up the ramp. She wanted a few minutes to see everything before Aunt Joyce saw her.

Aunt Joyce still matched the picture Birdie carried in her head from the last time she'd seen her years ago. Short white hair, round face, light-brown-rimmed glasses, a mole on her cheek, the trace of a mustache on her lip, and lots of freckles. Now Aunt Joyce's white hair stuck out from under a funny little rain hat that looked even odder because of the sunshine streaming through the terminal's windows behind her. A solid chunk of woman, wide through the waist and shoulders without being really fat, Aunt Joyce didn't seem to notice the businessmen and vacationers pushing past her as she intently studied a slip of paper in her hand and then each person who came up the exit ramp.

When at last the two businessmen in front of Birdie parted and revealed Birdie to her aunt's eyes, relief flooded Aunt Joyce's face, changing the worry lines around her eyes to smile lines.

Once she had been spotted, Birdie clutched her canvas bag and waited for her aunt to make her way through the crowd over to her. It took a long time, because instead of pushing through people, Aunt Joyce waited for pathways to open. She'd never survive in the city, Birdie thought without moving forward to meet her halfway.

"Birdie?" Aunt Joyce said when she finally reached her. "You remember me, don't you? Your Aunt Joyce?" Her aunt smiled, but a lot of doubt showed in her watery green eyes, which were slightly magnified by the lenses of her glasses. Birdie wasn't sure if she was getting ready to cry or simply had allergies.

"I remember," Birdie said. She told herself she ought to smile so that her aunt would feel better, but Birdie's mouth stayed tight. She didn't have time for acting right now. She had to figure everything out first. Besides, she didn't want to look too eager. It hadn't been her idea to come to Aunt Joyce, and it wouldn't last long. Nothing ever did.

"Well, I didn't know," Aunt Joyce said, some of the doubt slipping down from her eyes into her voice. "It's been a long time. Nearly seven years. You couldn't have been much over five."

"I was almost six, and you came to see Kevin. He was five months old and just starting to sit up. He had two teeth, and you wore a beige sweater with a couple of black sheep on the front up around the neck. You gave my mother one like it that was green without the sheep and you had made Kevin a blue blanket. Before you left, you said you'd make me a

2

sweater when you got home. It came in the mail right before we moved. I should have sent you a thank you note, but I didn't have a stamp. It was a nice sweater.''

Aunt Joyce backed up a little, her smile stiffening on her face as she listened to Birdie's recital. ''My, you certainly have a good memory.''

''Yes,'' Birdie said. She could have told her more about the sweater, about how it had been a bright pink with shiny white buttons down the front. Her mother had said the pink looked awful with Birdie's red hair, but Birdie had liked the bright color and worn it everywhere. She'd kept wearing it until the sleeves were halfway up to her elbows, and even after she'd quit wearing it, she'd kept it for a long time. She'd finally sold it to a neighbor for fifty cents. They'd needed milk.

Now she kept her mouth shut. There wasn't any need to tell Aunt Joyce all that. Birdie's mother always said she told too much.

Aunt Joyce's smile slipped completely away. She reached up and adjusted her plastic rain hat, then summoned the smile back up to try again. ''I wasn't so sure I'd recognize you, but I'd have known you even without your mother's description.'' She waved the piece of paper she still had in her hand before she tucked it into her huge handbag. ''That red hair of yours is just like mine used to be. And you've got almost as many freckles as I do.''

Birdie rubbed her hand across her face as though she could make the freckles disappear.

Aunt Joyce laughed. ''Freckles aren't so bad. At least you learn to live with them after a while. A good thing, too. I've got them everywhere.''

3

She held out her arms toward Birdie. Her freckles were so fat they almost touched. Birdie looked down at her own arms, where the freckles were neat dots of reddish brown with plenty of white skin still showing around them. She had the horrible thought that maybe her freckles would just keep growing forever, the way they said noses and ears did, and eventually take over her body. She pictured it in her mind, turning over the possibilities. It might not be so bad, she decided finally. In fact it might be better to be covered with one giant freckle instead of a zillion baby ones.

Aunt Joyce moved closer as if to hug her, but then just patted her shoulder before she said, "I guess we need to get your luggage."

"I've got it." Birdie held up her canvas bag.

"But I told your mother to let you bring whatever you wanted."

"This is enough," Birdie said. "I don't like having so many clothes I can't decide what to wear."

"That makes sense," Aunt Joyce said as she turned quickly away, but not before Birdie could see the pity flash through her eyes.

Birdie had been prepared for that, but pity didn't mean they liked her. It just meant they thought she was pitiful. Pushing the thought away, Birdie followed after her aunt. She could have gotten through the people twice as fast as Aunt Joyce, but she bit back her impatience and matched her pace to her aunt's. It wouldn't last, but for a while they'd both have to pretend it might.

She studied Aunt Joyce's back and thought about how she would describe her to Kevin. He'd been curious about this aunt he didn't know. Aunt Joyce would have taken him, too, but Kevin had a father,

4

Willie Baker, who wanted Kevin to stay with him while their mother was in the treatment center. It was part of the deal. Birdie's mother had to get treatment, Kevin would go to his father, and Birdie to anybody who would take her. The social worker had seen to it all.

Birdie felt a knot jump up in her throat when she thought about Kevin. She didn't know how he'd get along without her. Willie didn't know which stories he liked to hear at night and which teddy bear he had to sleep with. Kevin knew, she told herself before the knot could dissolve into tears. He could tell Willie.

"You okay back there?" Aunt Joyce asked with a smile over her shoulder. "We're almost to the door. Just a little farther. I can't imagine where all these people came from."

Birdie attempted something close to a smile, and Aunt Joyce seemed satisfied. She was nothing like Birdie's mother, even if they were sisters. Birdie's mother was thinner even than Birdie, with dark brown hair and long-fingered hands that trembled. Her mother's face looked tight, as though she were working hard at control, except of course when she was drinking. Then everything got too loose.

In contrast, everything about Aunt Joyce's face looked soft, gentle. Her backside was wide, but no flesh jiggled as she determinedly walked forward in a kind of stop, shift, move forward dance through the crowds. Once outside they walked faster and Aunt Joyce was panting a little by the time they got across the parking lot to her old blue station wagon. Still, her hands were rock-steady as she inserted the key in the lock.

"I hate driving in all this traffic," Aunt Joyce said

5

as she pulled out of the parking lot and squinted through her glasses at the signs. "Look for the sign that says east. I think it's east we need to go. At least I hope so."

Birdie pointed out the east sign and then held her breath as Aunt Joyce bounced out onto the highway. It didn't look like much traffic to Birdie, but Aunt Joyce was gripping the steering wheel while her eyes flashed back and forth between the rearview mirror and the road. She didn't say anything more until she asked Birdie to watch for the exit sign to Brookdale.

It was a huge sign nobody who wasn't blind could miss, but Birdie dutifully pointed it out. After they were out on the winding two-lane road, Aunt Joyce relaxed.

"I haven't driven to Louisville since my mother was in the hospital years ago. They've changed the roads all around since then." She glanced over at Birdie, who was staring out at the farmland flowing past the windows. "You remember Grandma, don't you?"

"Yes." Birdie pulled her eyes away from the side of the road to look at her aunt. "I stayed with her two months, but then she got sick and died. My mother said it must have been too hard on her taking care of me."

"I don't think that had anything to do with it, Birdie. Your grandmother just got old. It happens to us all," Aunt Joyce said with a sigh.

Birdie looked at her and wondered how old she was, but she didn't ask.

Aunt Joyce shook herself a little. "Of course you're too young to worry about getting old. When you're thirteen, you want to get older and fast."

Birdie turned her eyes back to the side of the road. She'd been here before. She remembered the way the green grass ran across the fields to solid banks of trees in the distance. Still, she felt somehow alien to it all, as if she had landed on some new, strange world she had yet to obtain enough information about to know how she should act.

Now that Aunt Joyce wasn't having to concentrate on her driving, she chattered first about one thing, then another. Birdie half listened as she kept her eyes on the roadside. She noted every house, tree, and cow. Her mother often told her she was too much like a computer, absorbing everything around her as so much data.

"You'll start school on Monday. I've already talked to Mr. Wright, who's the principal there at the middle school, and Mrs. Hansen is supposed to send your school records," Aunt Joyce was saying. "That nice Mrs. Hansen says you're an excellent student as far as grades are concerned, but that you've always missed too many days."

Mrs. Hansen was the social worker, the woman who held Kevin and Birdie's future in her hands. Birdie didn't look at Aunt Joyce as she said, "Mama was sick a lot. I had to take care of Kevin."

"Sick." The word seemed to almost choke Aunt Joyce, and she had to clear her throat before she could go on. "Well, she'll get better in the hospital. Mrs. Hansen says it's a good program and that they have a high success rate."

"Yes," Birdie agreed.

"A few months and then your mother will be just fine again," Aunt Joyce said, but her voice sounded far from sure.

7

Birdie turned herself into a computer again and let Aunt Joyce's words clatter through her mind.

"However long it takes though, you don't have to worry, Birdie. You can stay with me and Uncle Albert."

I-t w-o-n-'-t l-a-s-t. The words clicked through Birdie's head one letter at a time.

Aunt Joyce was still talking. "I'm sorry about that other time. You know, when your grandmother got sick. I just couldn't keep you then, not and take care of her, too, and with Susan and Andy still home. It was just too much."

"That's all right," Birdie heard herself saying.

"But the woman who came to get you assured me you were going to a nice family. She said they always screened all their foster families carefully."

"Yes," Birdie said as she began counting the brick houses they passed. They looked like big shoeboxes, sitting one next to another in a row along the road. She imagined them stacked one on top of the other like an apartment house in the city and all the extra land that would free for grass and trees and flowers. She didn't think about the foster families, even the one that had been nice. She'd stayed with three different ones until Kevin had been born and her mother had arranged for her to come home.

Leaving the shoebox houses behind, they drove through what Aunt Joyce called a town, where she pointed out the school, a small two-story building with rows of windows poked open. No air conditioning, Birdie thought. A flag waved from a flagpole. A line of teachers' cars was parked by a yellow school bus. There was nothing to see to prepare Birdie for

8

her first steps through the door into the hallway on the coming Monday.

Birdie stared hard at the building while she pictured all sorts and sizes of boys and girls inside at their desks. Big and little, short and tall, dumb and smart, but she didn't hold out much hope that any of them would be like her. At every school she'd ever been to, no matter how big and with how many students, she'd always stood out as different. It was her computer eyes, her mother told her. Nobody wanted to be friends with a computer.

It didn't matter anyway, Birdie thought. She wouldn't be here long, because it wouldn't last. Nothing ever did.

Finally they were turning up a long driveway which led to an old white house. A big porch spanned the front, and paint was peeling on the eaves. In the front yard a goat nibbled on ankle-high grass.

"Maybelle's our lawn mower," Aunt Joyce said with a laugh. "Just don't leave anything you value laying around the yard. She's a pretty good garbage disposal unit as well."

"Maybelle?"

"The goat. I always give all the animals names. It makes them more like family, you know. But come on. You'll want to see your room."

Aunt Joyce pushed a duck away from the front door. "That's Dumbo," she said as she threw open the door that hadn't even been locked.

"I thought Dumbo was an elephant," Birdie said as she followed Aunt Joyce.

"Not around here. Around here it's Dumbo the duck, and let me assure you the name fits."

Birdie stared at the duck quacking and waddling

toward the porch steps. As it tried to go down them, the duck upended on its beak, its legs and tail flounced out behind it. Birdie couldn't keep from smiling.

"Poor Dumbo," Aunt Joyce said. She went back out on the porch and set the duck down on the ground. "He's always had something wrong with his balance, but he just keeps on climbing up on the porch and then falling on his beak and quacking until I set him off. Your Uncle Albert says we should have had duck stew a long time ago."

Aunt Joyce came back up the steps and into the house, a little out of breath again. She led Birdie past a large, comfortable living room and down a hall out to an even bigger kitchen, where an old-fashioned spinning wheel sat in front of a wall of windows. Wire racks spilled over with all colors of yarn, and a basket with the beginnings of a red sweater sat by an armless rocking chair.

"That's my work corner," Aunt Joyce said. "It's a mess, but if I clean it up I can't find anything." She flipped over to the stove and turned on a burner under a big black kettle. She looked comfortable and totally at ease for the first time. "I hope you like soup."

"We ate soup a lot at home," Birdie said.

"Your mother made soup?" Aunt Joyce sounded surprised.

"We just opened cans. It's easier that way."

"I suppose it is. Albert says I do everything the hard way."

"I've never eaten homemade soup," Birdie said.

"Poor dear." Aunt Joyce reached out and put her arm around Birdie. Although they were very near the

10

same height, Aunt Joyce was at least three times as wide. When Aunt Joyce tightened her arm in a hug, Birdie couldn't keep from stiffening a little. Aunt Joyce didn't act as if she noticed. She just hugged quickly and turned loose. "There's probably going to be a lot of firsts for you around here after living all your life in a big city, but maybe it won't be too strange for you."

"It won't be strange," Birdie said. "It feels homey." She wasn't sure why she said that. It was a mistake, even if it did make Aunt Joyce beam. There was no use getting either of their hopes up, because it wouldn't last. But Birdie had never been in a room like this, with its quilted duck and pig pictures and brooms decorated with dried flowers hanging on the walls. It did feel homey.

Aunt Joyce was giving her directions to the bathroom and to her room upstairs. "We fixed up the spare room for you. It's sort of stuck out back here over the kitchen. Maybe years ago, when they had such things, it was the maid's room. Anyway, there's the stairway over there."

Birdie looked at the door in the corner Aunt Joyce was pointing out.

"Why don't you run on up and see how you like it?" Aunt Joyce said. "I used to have my workroom up there until my knees set up a constant fuss over all the climbing up and down, and those stairs are narrow. So watch your step."

As Birdie ran up the small, curving staircase, the door banged shut behind her. The privacy that door gave her made the room more than acceptable even before she reached the top of the stairs and came out

11

into the little room that looked like something out of a storybook.

A patchwork quilt covered the bed with an explosion of colors, and plump, white, ruffled pillows were propped against the headboard. Against the opposite wall there was a dresser with a large, round mirror that wobbled a bit as Birdie walked across the floor toward it. She barely glanced at her reflection before turning to the window, where a slight breeze ruffled the white curtains and sunshine streamed through to warm the top of a small desk.

As wonderful as the desk was, even more amazing was the cat in the middle of the bed. A real cat. It sat up at the sight of Birdie and stretched. When Birdie reached out a hand to hesitantly touch it, the cat punched its head up in her palm and arched its back through a long body rub. Its purring vibrated against Birdie's hand.

Almost without thinking, she picked up the cat and held it close to her face. It was nothing like the strays that had hung out behind the apartment house ready to pounce on any scrap of food and skulking away suspiciously at the first sign of affection. This cat lay back in her hands, completely content.

It was an ugly, mottled black and gray with yellow and white patches mixed in. One ear was half gone, and the other stuck up funny. Its head, round and pointy, somehow didn't seem to fit the rest of its body.

"You've got to be the ugliest cat I've ever seen," Birdie said even as a smile spread across her face. The cat purred louder. "And you don't even know it."

Birdie pulled herself up short. No way was she

going to let herself get attached to a cat and have to feel sad when she left. She was just here to sleep and eat a while until they sent her somewhere else to sleep and eat a while before she got to go back and be with her mother and Kevin.

She was starting toward the stairway to take the cat down to the kitchen when she heard Aunt Joyce clambering up the narrow steps.

"Is the room okay?" Aunt Joyce asked when she got to the top. Then she spotted the cat in Birdie's hands. "So this is where Kat was hiding this morning. She sneaks away every time she thinks I'm getting ready to put her outside. Bad Kat." But Aunt Joyce was smiling as she reached over and touched the cat's head.

"Cat? I thought you said all the animals had names."

"They do. Kat is K-a-t. She was a stray that just showed up at the door one day, and she was so scrawny with her ear hanging down bleeding that I honestly didn't think she'd live, and Albert didn't really want me to keep her, so I just sort of halfway named her." Aunt Joyce gently stroked the cat again. "But she didn't die, and even if she isn't the prettiest cat in the world, she grows on you after a while."

"I don't want her up here."

"Why not? Kat won't hurt anything. She just likes to sleep on beds and sometimes look at herself in mirrors. I think she's wishing for another cat as ugly as she is."

Birdie felt a smile want to start inside her, but she didn't let it out. Instead she dropped the cat on the floor. "I don't like cats. I might even be allergic to them."

Aunt Joyce looked at her with doubt in her eyes, but she only said, "Then I guess Kat better sleep on someone else's bed." She reached down to catch the cat, but Kat shot under the bed. "Here, kitty, kitty," Aunt Joyce called, but the cat wouldn't come out.

After a few minutes, Aunt Joyce straightened up and said, "She'll come out when it's time to eat, and then if you keep the door to the stairs closed she might not get back up here."

"Okay," Birdie said.

Aunt Joyce was quiet a minute before she asked, "Other than Kat, is the room okay? I didn't put up anything on the walls. I thought maybe you'd want to do that yourself, and Uncle Albert is making you some shelves."

"The room's very nice," Birdie said. "Thank you."

Aunt Joyce floundered around for more to say. She told Birdie that Uncle Albert would be home from driving the school bus soon, and then after he fed the animals they'd eat supper and after that she could watch television or do whatever she was used to doing.

Birdie listened without helping much, and finally Aunt Joyce said, "We want you to feel at home here and be happy."

"Thank you," Birdie said politely.

Before she went back down to the kitchen, Aunt Joyce tried one last time to get Kat to come out from under the bed, but it was no use.

"It's okay. I don't care if she stays under the bed," Birdie said.

"Well, if she comes out, you can chase her down to the kitchen."

14

After Birdie heard the door downstairs bang lightly shut behind Aunt Joyce, she went over to the desk in front of the window. Pens and pencils, school paper, and a couple of notebooks lay on top. She ran her finger down one of the notebook's ring binder and then smoothed her hand across its shiny red cover.

It won't last, she whispered to herself. Besides, she didn't want to stay here. Not really. She wanted to be with Kevin. He needed her to take care of him.

Birdie looked out over the green fields where a lot of woolly sheep and a few cows had their noses to the ground. Then she spotted a funny-looking, long-necked animal sauntering along the fence. Birdie searched through her memory for the right name. Llama. It was a llama, but what was it doing on Aunt Joyce's farm? Llamas belonged in South America.

Again, as she stared at the exotic-looking animal, Birdie had the feeling she'd been dropped down in a strange new world.

She sat down at the desk and picked up one of the pens. She'd promised not only to write Kevin and tell him all about Aunt Joyce and Uncle Albert, but also to write him stories like the kind she sometimes told him at bedtime.

She wrote *Dear Kevin*, and then stopped. She wasn't sure yet exactly what she wanted to say about Aunt Joyce, and she hadn't even met Uncle Albert. So she skipped on to the story.

"Galiena had been on the new, strange planet for three hours, twenty minutes, sixteen and one-half seconds. If she was lucky and kept anyone from finding out she was an alien, she had two months to discover the secrets of this new world,

15

but they promised to be two months of unimaginable dangers. Galiena wished she could go back to her spaceship and return to Theopolis with the rest of the crew, but she had a mission.''

The ugly cat came out from under the bed, hopped up on the desk, and curled up half on the notebook. When Birdie touched the cat's head, her hand jerked forth an immediate purring response. Birdie eased the notebook out from under Kat and continued to write.

"Galiena had found one true friend on this strange world. The one-eyed creature called a cat reminded Galiena of the gentle katuras on Theopolis that lived to bring pleasure to their owners. Still this creature was different. Its coat was camouflaged for night hunting, and it claimed to be able to see through the darkness. It slept through the sun hours and waited for the night, when it promised to help Galiena search out the answers she needed to complete her mission. Galiena named the creature Katura. It liked its name.

"All around them were unknown dangers. Galiena had to learn the ways of this strange world quickly, and there was only Katura to guide her."

16

Chapter 2

The next morning at breakfast, when Uncle Albert said he needed to go to town to get gasoline for his tractor, Aunt Joyce told him she and Birdie would feed the animals.

Birdie looked up from her plate of scrambled eggs, sausage, and biscuits. In the two meals she'd had with Aunt Joyce and Uncle Albert, she'd been expected to eat more food than she'd seen in two weeks. Birdie pushed her eggs back and forth with her fork and wondered if she dared ask Aunt Joyce if she had any cornflakes.

"You don't mind, do you, Birdie? I mean helping with the animals," Aunt Joyce said after Uncle Albert left.

"No. I expect to have chores. I'll start with the dishes if you want." Birdie carried her plate to the sink. There were still lots of eggs on it, but she couldn't eat any more.

"Dishes can wait," Aunt Joyce said. She opened a closet, and after exchanging her house shoes for rubber boots and slapping a straw hat on her head, she looked critically at Birdie's white sneakers. "Do you have other shoes to wear to school?"

"There's nothing wrong with these," Birdie said.

"There might be something wrong with them if you wear them out to do the chores." Aunt Joyce handed Birdie a pair of dirty sneakers with holes in the toes. "These might be a little big for you, but they'll have to do till we can go shopping."

While Birdie pulled on the stiff shoes, Aunt Joyce scraped up the remains of breakfast in a big pan. "Reever will think it's Christmas morning."

Reever turned out to be a sad-eyed basset hound whose ears lapped at the ground when he walked to meet Aunt Joyce, while his tail wagged slowly back and forth as though each wag was a kind of salute. Then they fed the barn cats, Pickin and Grinnin. Birdie wasn't sure which was which. Two calves had to be bottle-fed, and after Aunt Joyce mixed their feed, she handed Birdie one of the bottles. The little calf named Winnie knocked the plastic bottle out of Birdie's hands twice before she figured out how to grip it tightly enough.

By the time they left the barn and Aunt Joyce was introducing the sheep one by one, Birdie's head was whirling with names. Blackie, Herb, Jolene, Bertha. When the llama sauntered over their way, Birdie began to feel like Galiena, the character in her story to Kevin. Her airplane must have really been a spaceship taking her to another world.

"This is Cleopatra," Aunt Joyce said as she reached out tentatively toward the haughty head of the animal. "She's a bit temperamental, but her wool makes such interesting sweaters and blankets."

The llama endured Aunt Joyce's touch, but when Birdie put out her hand, it pulled back its head and spit. Aunt Joyce yanked Birdie to the side so that

18

only a bit of the llama's saliva spattered on Birdie's arm. It smelled awful.

Aunt Joyce began mopping at Birdie's arm with a handkerchief. "I should have warned you, Birdie. I'm sorry." Aunt Joyce glanced over at the llama. "Cleopatra is so bad. She spits at everybody the first time she sees them, and then she stands back and laughs."

Birdie looked at the llama, who did seem to be smirking, with her head high, her eyes glinting, and her lips twitching up and down over her teeth. "She doesn't bite, too, does she?"

"No, she only spits, but that's bad enough. It smells horrible. I'm afraid if you got any on your clothes, you'll just have to change right away. The smell sort of lingers." Aunt Joyce held her handkerchief away from her and made a face.

"Is she going to spit at me every time I get close?" Birdie backed up as the llama stepped closer to the fence.

"Only until you convince her to like you."

"But I don't care whether she likes me or not."

"Then you'd better stay out of spitting range. Cleopatra thinks she's the queen around here. If you don't pay homage, then watch out."

As they walked back toward the house, Birdie glanced back over her shoulder at the llama, who was swaying her head back and forth on her long neck. Galiena had met her first planetary monster. That would make Kevin happy. He liked monsters in all his stories.

"Maybelle just can't keep up with the grass," Aunt Joyce was saying as they waded through the tall

19

grass toward the house. "I guess we're going to have to get the lawnmower out."

"Can I do it?" Birdie asked. She looked down at the grass and then remembered all the houses they'd passed on the way to the farm. They all had yards. "Maybe I could even get some jobs mowing other yards, too."

"Oh, you don't have to do that."

"Why not? I knew this boy once who made lots of money mowing around banks and in the suburbs. His grandmother lived out there."

"You don't have to work, Birdie. We'll give you spending money," Aunt Joyce said.

"I had a job at home."

"What kind of job?" Aunt Joyce asked as though she weren't sure she wanted to hear the answer.

"At a gas station. Sweeping up mostly, but sometimes I pumped the gas if everybody else was busy."

"You're too young to worry about having a job."

"Mama said she worked on the farm when she was growing up. That she had to chop weeds and pick beans and tomatoes."

"That's different," Aunt Joyce said.

"So is mowing yards," Birdie argued. "I'll be getting sunshine and exercise and staying busy and out of trouble."

She thought maybe she'd made one argument too many when Aunt Joyce's eyes narrowed, but her aunt only said, "We'll see what your uncle thinks when he gets back from town."

Uncle Albert must have thought it was a good idea, because he got the lawnmower out of the garage and showed Birdie how to start it up. He said hard work never hurt anybody. It just kept them too tired to get into trouble.

Birdie looked up at him when he said that. He was poking around in the garage, hunting for a jug to pour gasoline in for the mower. He wasn't very tall, only an inch or two taller than Birdie, and his stomach lapped over his belt a little from all of Aunt Joyce's good cooking. His head was bald on top, and he must not have shaved that morning, because Birdie could see his black and gray whiskers. At supper the night before he'd smiled at Birdie a time or two, but he'd let Aunt Joyce do all the talking, only occasionally mumbling an all-purpose sound as a kind of punctuation mark to Aunt Joyce's words. He hadn't seemed to mind Birdie being there.

But now the way he said trouble made Birdie sigh inwardly and wonder what Mrs. Hansen had told them about her. There was nothing to do but come right out with it and clear the air. She waited until he turned back around. Then she looked at him directly as she said, "I won't get into any kind of trouble while I'm here. That's a promise, and I keep my promises."

Uncle Albert dropped his eyes to the antifreeze jug he'd found and began rubbing the dust off its top. "I wasn't meaning you would," he mumbled. "That's just what my daddy used to tell me about working. Me and your Aunt Joyce are glad enough to have you here with us as long as you want to stay."

All those words coming out of his mouth seemed to surprise both of them, and Birdie wished she'd let it pass without saying anything. She'd figured on him nodding solemnly and accepting her promise. That's all. But then grown-ups were sometimes hard to figure.

Uncle Albert cleared his throat as he screwed the top off the antifreeze bottle and peered inside. "This ought to do."

The uncomfortable moment was past, and Uncle Albert again kept his eyes somewhere in the air just the other side of her face as he told her where to find a funnel.

Birdie thought it only fair that she mow their yard first, before she went out hunting customers. As she made the first round of the yard and watched the grass fly out behind her, leaving a smooth, even strip, Birdie began to calculate her possible earnings.

She'd save all she could. That way no matter what else happened she'd still have a way to go back to see Kevin. She could even send Kevin some of the money so he could buy baseball cards and bubblegum and other things he needed for school. Things Willie might not think about.

Thinking of Kevin made Birdie feel better. No matter what else happened, she and Kevin could always depend on one another. They were family in a way that could never be changed. Husbands and wives got divorced. Sometimes fathers or mothers gave their children up for adoption, but sisters and brothers had a special bond even the social workers recognized. Birdie had seen the pictures in the paper of families of sisters and brothers trying to find adoptive homes.

Not that she and Kevin had to worry about that. Kevin had a father, and they both had a mother. Of course Birdie had a father, too, somewhere. Avery Honaker. She was named after him and her Aunt Joyce. Avery Joyce Honaker. But her mother hadn't liked the names after she'd put them on the birth certificate.

Birdie didn't know where her nickname came from. She just knew Birdie was what she'd always been called. In fact she hadn't even known her name was Avery until the social worker carted her off to the first foster family and everyone had begun calling her that. Even then she hadn't realized her name was actually Avery. She'd thought the foster family had simply renamed her. It was only after the next family called her Avery, too, that she realized the name must be some part of her identity.

She hadn't told the families she was really called Birdie. It was a secret she wrapped herself in. That way when the bad times came she could retreat into her secret identity and nothing they said or did touched the real Birdie.

Birdie had never quite given up her secret identity after that, even when she returned home and people began calling her Birdie again. It didn't pay to depend too much on anybody else. It was better to keep a secret place inside.

Now, as she made the rounds of the yard, she wrapped the noise of the lawnmower around her and enjoyed the isolation that gave her. She could look out and see all the world around her, but she couldn't be expected to respond in any way.

That was going to be the hardest part of living with Aunt Joyce and Uncle Albert. Staying apart. They were nice. It was always harder to stay in her separate place when the people were nice, but she didn't have any choice. It wouldn't last. It never did. So it was easier just to keep herself apart to begin with.

Still, staying here a few weeks or months might

not be so bad. It was the middle of September. There'd be a few more weeks of yard mowing before the weather turned cold. Besides, she'd no doubt be gone by then anyway.

That's the way she wanted it. Back with Kevin. Until then she could make a little money in a job that was perfect for her purposes. The mower was loud enough that it shut her away from the world without shutting out what she could see. She'd be like Galiena, here from another planet to investigate the unique properties of the new one.

As she kept turning the corners of the yard, she began to think about Galiena's story.

"Galiena had found the perfect place for her stay on the new world. The old couple were kindly but not of the suspicious sort. They'd believe whatever she told them. That was good.

"Already she'd begun studying the different creatures she'd seen, making detailed notes of the way they looked while she searched her memory for comparison with creatures of her home planet. There were the harmless creatures, the basset hound and the goat, although Katura, her ally on this strange world, was not that sure the basset was harmless, in spite of his floppy ears and slow movements. But they were agreed about the monster llama.

"It was not huge, but there was a wicked glint in its eyes and Galiena feared it held secret powers in reserve. The kindly old woman had been fooled into thinking the creature was some sort of queen. But Galiena saw through its disguise and into its evil heart.

24

"She shuddered at the thought, but she knew she was going to have to find out more about this monster. It was part of her mission. Plus there were surely other monsters yet to be discovered.

"Galiena missed her home and her friends on Theopolis, but she had to complete her mission. She had to get to know the people here and discover their secrets without letting them guess her true identity."

By the time Birdie had made the last round of the yard and it lay all around her like a smooth, green carpet, she felt almost as if she'd actually become Galiena, and as she went down the driveway and up the road, excitement tickled awake inside her. She was going to search out the secrets of this strange place.

The first houses she came to were set apart off the highway on another road guarded by a rock entrance and a large sign that declared this was Lionhaven Heights.

Although Birdie bravely walked through the impressive posts with stone lions crouched on top, it took her a few minutes to work up the courage to approach the first house. No one answered the doorbell, but the yard was neatly mowed and trimmed already. At the next house the yard was shaggier, but the woman there said they did their own mowing. Birdie wasn't discouraged. She'd counted twelve houses on the street. If she could get two yards today, she'd be happy.

At the fifth house, a middle-aged woman looked at her doubtfully, asked who she was, and hired her without another question when she found out she was staying with Albert and Joyce Moore.

"Your aunt has knitted sweaters for all my grand-children. You can't find a nicer woman." Mrs. McCulley looked at Birdie with a smile that trusted by association. After they worked out the when and how much of their mowing agreement, Birdie moved on up the street with Mrs. McCulley's smile still beaming strong behind her.

The next house wasn't the biggest on the street, but Birdie had been aware of it since she first started down the line of the houses because of its stately air. It sat at the end of the road, facing not toward the other houses but sort of to the side, as if it didn't acknowledge the presence of its neighbors. Even the trees and bushes in the yard seemed bigger, lusher, and more established in their places than the trees in the other lawns.

"Grass is grass," Birdie whispered to herself as she walked up the circular, concrete drive toward the front door that was flanked by narrow strips of gold-colored glass. "And money is money."

Birdie was about to press the doorbell when she heard the thump of a basketball pounding against con-crete and then the rattle of a goal as a shot bounced away. The familiar city sounds seemed out of place at this awesome house, where Birdie wouldn't have been surprised if a uniformed maid had answered the door.

Birdie pulled her finger away from the doorbell and went around the side of the house toward the sound of the ball slapping concrete. At the corner of the house, she stopped and watched a boy about her age dribble a basketball back and forth across a driveway

26

that blimped out toward the goal on the side. His concentration was so intense as he attacked the goal that he didn't notice her there.

The boy wasn't very tall, and he wore dark-rimmed glasses secured with a red strap that showed up brightly against his short brown hair. Still, as he put up shots that often missed the rim entirely as they bounded off the backboard, Birdie knew that inside his head he was imagining himself to be one of the pros saving a game with a last-second desperation shot.

In her head she added him to Galiena's finds. He could be Galiena's first human friend, even though Katura would warn Galiena against him.

Birdie made no move to give her presence away, but finally the boy turned and caught sight of her there. He let the ball roll away from him as he asked, "What are you doing here?"

"Watching you," Birdie answered.

Frowning, he retrieved the ball before he asked suspiciously, "Where did you come from?"

"Theopolis," Birdie answered without thinking.

Chapter 3

He didn't laugh at her, although boys often did. They looked at the beanpole-skinny girl with her red hair and freckles, and when she returned their look with a peculiarly direct stare, they didn't know what else to do but laugh in hopes that it would keep her from seeing through them so completely.

It never did, because Birdie knew how to watch for a change in the eyes, a shuffling of the feet, a twitch of the hands, or a tilt of the head. More times than not, she could guess what they were getting ready to say or do.

Now she waited as the boy peered at her through glasses that were steaming up and considered her foolish answer. She nearly smiled when his eyes took on a glazed look that meant he was no longer really seeing her but was shuffling through information in his head to come up with a proper reply. Then she wanted to laugh out loud, not because anything was funny, but because she realized that here in front of her was someone else her mother would have said had computer eyes. It was all she could do to keep standing still and continue to watch him without any change of her expression while she thought about the possibility of knowing someone who might be like her.

Finally he took off his glasses, rubbed them off on his shorts, and put them back on before he said, "There is no place called Theopolis."

"No known place," she said with only the hint of a knowing smile. "I come from a galaxy far, far away."

He still didn't smile. "Then I suppose you want me to take you to my leader."

"Do you have a leader?"

"Only my mother, and somehow I doubt she'd be impressed with your story. She's more into Shakespeare and Hemingway than science fiction."

Birdie let her smile spread across her face and dropped the story. "Actually, I've just moved in down the road and I'm looking for jobs mowing yards." She looked away from him at the lawn. "I don't suppose you need someone."

"Unfortunately not. My mother seems to think I myself am supremely qualified for the job."

"I figured as much, but it never hurts to ask." Birdie hesitated a moment, half hoping he'd ask her to shoot some baskets with him, but he just kept staring at her as though she really had come from a place called Theopolis. He didn't seem to recognize that they were meant to be friends. Somehow she'd have to find a way to feed that information to him.

"Well, thanks anyway," she said as she half turned to go. "I don't guess you can give me any leads about your neighbors on this side of the street. I've already asked on that side." Birdie pointed.

"Girls don't mow yards for other people. They get jobs baby-sitting."

"Mowing's easier and more fun."

"You don't like babies?"

"Some of them." Birdie turned all the way back around to look at him. "How about you? Do you like babies?"

"I don't know any. At least not personally," the boy said. "But there are lots of them around here, so it shouldn't be hard to find somebody who needs a baby-sitter."

"Then maybe you should get a job baby-sitting."

"I have a job already."

"What? Mowing this yard and shooting baskets? Or maybe studying is your job." Birdie watched his eyes closely to see if she'd been successful in making him mad.

If her half-taunts bothered him, he didn't show it. "I work at a nature sanctuary down the road."

"That's nice," Birdie said. "Animal-sitting is probably easier than baby-sitting any day."

"It depends on the animal you're sitting," the boy said. "Take Ralph there." He pointed at a huge yellow cat stretched out in the sunshine next to the door. At the sound of his name, the cat flipped up the very end of his tail one time only, as if that was all the energy he had to expend. "He's easy to sit."

"Yeah, I guess so. And I have to admit I wouldn't want to baby-sit a llama."

"A llama?" The look on his face shifted, and Birdie grinned a little. She'd managed to get a reaction, finally.

"Yeah," she said casually. "See you around."

"Wait," he said as she started off. "If you really want a job, Mike—he's the boss down at the sanctuary—sometimes hires kids to mow around the

30

parking area and such. But he's particular. Most kids mow once and quit or get fired."

"What's the name of the place?"

"The Burton Riggs Sanctuary for Birds and Small Animals."

"What a name," Birdie said. "How far away is it?"

"About a mile on down the road. I ride my bike."

"You work every day?"

"Sometimes, if Mike needs me, but mostly on weekends."

"I see," Birdie said. "Thanks for the tip. I'll check into it."

"No thanks needed. Mike probably won't hire a girl anyway," the boy said as he began bouncing the basketball again.

"Yeah, well, you never know," Birdie said. "See you around sometime, maybe."

"In a town the size of Brookdale, that's not only a possibility, it's a definite probability."

It wasn't one he sounded as if he looked forward to as he turned away from her and threw up the basketball. When the shot bounced off to the left, Birdie could barely keep from offering him some advice about improving his shooting form, but she'd never met a boy yet who liked a girl to tell him how to play ball. So she kept her mouth shut and left.

As she walked back down his driveway, Birdie decided she was glad he hadn't been friendlier. She'd always been suspicious of people who were too friendly before they even knew anything about her. Besides, it would probably be better if she just forgot the strange feeling that the two of them were meant to be friends. He hadn't felt it or he would have at least told her his name or asked her hers. Of course she'd find out about him whether he told her anything or not. She had her ways.

Just watching him play ball and talking to him had told her a lot of things. He was smarter than he was athletic. He wished he could stretch his slightly tubby body into a lean, muscular build. He hated wearing glasses, and whether he had a job or not, his family had plenty of money, because he was wearing brand-new, expensive hightops just to shoot baskets out back behind his house. Last, but not least, he was suspicious of girls who liked science fiction and went about hunting yard-mowing jobs.

Birdie looked back when she got to the end of the drive, but she couldn't see him now, although she could still faintly hear the thump of the basketball. She smiled. Before she left Brookdale, she would play a basketball game with him, one on one. And she would win. That would be his punishment for not telling her his name.

She and a kid named Harry had played ball in the city. Harry, who was four inches taller, usually won, but sometimes Birdie could sneak a winning shot in with a quick fake and some fancy footwork that wasn't entirely according to official game rules. As a team they'd never been beaten on their dirt court out behind her apartment building. Still, though they had slapped hands and punched shoulders, they hadn't been talking friends. Birdie didn't even know where Harry lived, and she hadn't had the chance to tell him she was leaving.

She wasn't too worried about it. Harry would wonder where she was a time or two when he came to shoot baskets, but then he'd find a new ball-playing partner. He wouldn't wonder about her too much. Where they lived in the city, people came and went all the time.

Here it was different, Birdie thought as she went from one house to the next. That kid back there with his fancy private basketball goal had probably lived in that big, fine house for years. He probably not only had his own bedroom but his own bathroom as well.

Birdie got her second job at the last house on the street. A man was mowing, but when she approached him, he gladly handed over the mower on the spot. She finished the job and then headed back to Aunt Joyce's with money in her pocket.

The money made her feel good. She had gotten two yards, just the way she'd planned when she started out. And she'd get the job at that animal sanctuary place, too.

After supper that night while she was helping with the dishes, she asked Aunt Joyce about it.

"Oh yes, it's just down the road a little ways. A nice place, but then I like birds."

"Have you been there a lot?"

"Not lately. I guess when Joe Burton Riggs first donated the land to the county in memory of his father, with plenty of money to keep it going, we were all a little curious about exactly what he had planned down there. How did you find out about it? Did you go down there today? Is that why you were gone so long this afternoon?" Aunt Joyce's voice was carefully casual.

Birdie quickly looked over at Aunt Joyce and then back down at the suds in the sink. Birdie had known both Aunt Joyce and Uncle Albert were upset about something as soon as she'd gotten back to the house that afternoon, but until now she hadn't known what.

As Birdie rinsed a glass till it sparkled, she remembered how Aunt Joyce had flung open the door before Birdie had even reached the porch, and how Uncle Albert had been peering out the window at her. Even Kat had jumped down off the couch to come hurrying over to greet her.

Now Birdie realized with a start that they'd been worried about her. She was surprised it had taken her so long to figure it out, but at home she'd come and gone when she wished. As long as she made sure Kevin was taken care of, her mother never noticed if she was late or not. Actually, there was no late, because there was no schedule unless Birdie made it. The last few months after her mother had lost her job at the insurance office, her mother's only schedule had been from one drink to the next.

Birdie had shamelessly used Kevin to coax their mother to eat, to change clothes, and to go to bed. Kevin could look at their mother with tears pooling in his solemn brown eyes and get her to do anything he asked.

But now, here at Aunt Joyce's, it appeared there was a schedule that Birdie would have to learn to keep Aunt Joyce and Uncle Albert from worrying. Birdie concentrated on this new feeling of being worried about. She wasn't sure she liked it and even less sure she understood exactly why they'd been worried. Were they afraid she'd somehow gotten hurt or lost, or were they simply afraid she'd run off and they didn't know what they were supposed to do about it? Birdie decided this last must have been it, because nobody had had time to start liking anybody.

34

She glanced up at Aunt Joyce again as she set the glass in the drainer. There were worry lines around Aunt Joyce's eyes that her smile didn't hide. She was so nice, and she was trying so hard. Birdie determined right then to try to figure out their rules and to abide by them as much as possible until she had to leave.

She began by explaining where she'd been all afternoon and why she was late. "I told you I was going over to that bunch of houses up the road to see if I could get some yards to mow. And this one man wanted me to start right away." Birdie washed another glass and placed it just so in the drainer. "I didn't want to pass up the chance for a job."

"But you didn't have the mower with you," Aunt Joyce said as she spooned leftovers out of their big bowls into smaller bowls to make more dishes to wash up.

"I used his. I think he said his name was Johnson or Jackson or something like that. Then a Mrs. McCulley wants me to mow on Monday. She said she knew you."

"Well, it sounds as though your job hunting venture was successful," Aunt Joyce said with relief as the worry lines smoothed out around her eyes. "And Mrs. McCulley is a nice woman. Did she tell you about the sanctuary then?"

By now Birdie had washed all the glasses and was starting on the plates. One thing about a lot of food, it made a lot of dishes. Back at the apartment, sometimes the only dishes they had after a meal were the knife they used to spread the peanut butter on their bread, and their glasses, which they rinsed out and left by the sink until they wanted another drink.

"No, it wasn't Mrs. McCulley," Birdie said. "It was some boy at the house at the end of the street. You know, the one that sort of looks like it thinks it's better than all the rest of the houses."

Aunt Joyce stood still a minute to think, then laughed. "Why, yes, I guess I do know. The one with the antique looking brick?" When Birdie nodded, she went on. "That's the Riggs house, and you must have been talking to Jobee Riggs."

"Jobee?"

"A nickname, I suppose, because he's a junior, rather a third. Joseph Burton Riggs, III. It's a wonder he didn't tell you that if he told you about the sanctuary."

"He just said he worked there and that they sometimes hired people to do some mowing. I told him I was looking for some jobs."

"That was helpful of him. He's a nice little boy," Aunt Joyce said. "And awfully smart, but then he couldn't help but be smart with Dorothy and Joe Burton as parents. His father is the nearest thing we have to a famous person in Brookdale."

"Famous?" Birdie rinsed out the potato bowl. "What is he? Some kind of professional athlete or something?"

Aunt Joyce laughed again. "Oh no. Joe has made his fortune with his camera, traveling all over the world to take nature pictures for big magazines. He comes home for a week or two and then he's gone for months at a time. I don't know how Dorothy ever puts up with such an uncertain schedule."

Birdie didn't say anything as she began scrubbing the casserole bowl.

Aunt Joyce went on. "But then I guess she has

36

Lori and Jobee to take care of, and this year she's started teaching. If I'm not mistaken, I think she'll be your English teacher. That Dorothy," Aunt Joyce said and shook her head a little. "Her first year and already I've heard some of the mothers at church talking about her unusual methods."

"What do you mean?" Birdie asked as she attacked a pan with a scrub pad.

"Oh, I don't know. Just different than most teachers, but then Dorothy has always been a little different, always getting carried away by one enthusiasm, then another." Aunt Joyce dried the pan and shoved it down in the cabinet with a loud clatter. When she straightened back up, she said, "Why, once she even came to me for knitting lessons and tried to talk me into starting a cottage industry. And then there was the time she got the community theater to have a Shakespearean festival. That was a real disaster." Aunt Joyce laughed at the memory. "Anyway, I think the whole town is relieved that she's found a proper outlet for her energy that fits her talents."

"Yeah," Birdie said as she pulled the sink plug and let the water gurgle down the drain. "I guess she can quote Shakespeare all day to a captive audience."

"It won't hurt you young people to learn a little Shakespeare."

"Sounds like fun to me," Birdie said as she dried her hands on a tea towel. "But what about this Burton Riggs Sanctuary for Birds and Small Animals? What is it exactly?"

"Just what you said. It was old Mr. Riggs's farm, and after he died, Joe let it grow up wild. Then, once Joe had made a little money with his photographs, he turned it into an official sanctuary with a trust fund for its upkeep. They have paths through the woods so that maybe you can spot an animal here and there. Of course, they have birds everywhere. They even plant seed crops and cover for them.''

''What's there to mow then?''

''I'm trying to remember,'' Aunt Joyce said. ''They had an old log house that's been converted into a kind of museum with displays about wildlife. There's probably some yard around it that has to be mowed. I'm not real sure. It's been a while since I was down there.''

''You think it would be okay if I went tomorrow?'' Birdie wasn't used to asking permission to do things, and it somehow bothered her to do so now. Still, she'd decided to play by the rules, and she knew Aunt Joyce expected her to ask.

''I don't see why not. You've probably never been out in the woods like that. In fact, I think it would be a good idea.'' Aunt Joyce warmed to the idea as she took off her apron and hung it up. ''Albert can drive you down there after lunch tomorrow. By the way, dear, do you have anything you can wear to church in the morning?''

''Church?''

''Yes, dear, you'll have to attend church with us.''

Aunt Joyce's voice was firm, and Birdie knew that whatever else Aunt Joyce might have doubts about, this was one thing Birdie could not alter with any kind of argument or excuses. Birdie pulled a distressed face and tried an excuse anyway. ''I'm afraid I don't have any dresses, Aunt Joyce. Just jeans and shirts.''

''I thought that might be the case, so I found some material and made you a skirt this afternoon. I need

38

you to try it on before I do the hemming and put on the buttons.''

Later, after Aunt Joyce had taken up the waist of the skirt, clucking her tongue over how thin Birdie was, and pinned up the hem, Birdie escaped to her room. As soon as she opened the door to the stairs, Kat jumped off the couch and raced into the kitchen.

The cat seemed to have laid claim to Birdie. She'd sat in the window and watched her mow. She'd met Birdie at the door when she'd come back that afternoon, and she'd wound in and out between her legs while Birdie had washed the dishes. Now Aunt Joyce glanced up at them from her sewing machine, but she didn't say anything as Birdie let the cat leap lightly up the steps in front of her.

Once in her room, Birdie settled at the desk with her pen and notebook while Kat sat on the windowsill and stared out into the night. Birdie stared at the window for a moment as well, and then she began to write, easily picking up the thread of her story.

"Katura was anxious to begin her night explorations, but Galiena was hesitant to send her out, for she feared the unknown dangers in the night. There might be more monsters like the llama creature with the evil eyes. The mission was going well, and Galiena wanted to take no unnecessary risks.

"Just being here was risk enough. Galiena didn't like to think about what might happen to her if the natives found out she was an alien. They might even put her in a cage and study her, as legend had it they studied their little creatures called mice. It was said they used white mice. Galiena did not know. It was only one of the many things she must figure out about these strange people.

"She'd made her first contact with the native people other than the kindly couple who'd taken her in, never suspecting that she was an alien. She'd met a boy. He would be the gateway through which Galiena would go into this strange world to gather the needed information.

"Galiena had been on the planet twenty-eight hours, fourteen minutes, and eleven seconds."

Birdie lay down her pen, and Kat jumped down on the desk to push her head up into Birdie's hands. Birdie rubbed the cat as she looked at all the pages she'd written. Kevin wouldn't be able to read the story to himself. Even if she printed it all out, there would be too many words he didn't know.

With a sigh, she pushed the notebook aside and pulled out a sheet of the paper. "Dear Kevin," she printed carefully. "I hope you like your new place. I know you'll like being with Willie again. Aunt Joyce and Uncle Albert are real nice. They have a llama who spit at me. If you had seen it, you would have laughed. I'm writing you a story about a girl from outer space. I'll read it to you the next time I see you. Don't forget to do your homework and drink plenty of milk. Love, Birdie."

As she folded the note, she thought of Kevin with his straw-blond hair she could never get to lay down no matter how many times she wet the comb and tried. She remembered how his big brown eyes drank in her every expression when she told him stories.

Something squeezed inside her chest, and for a

40

minute she thought she might really cry, although she hadn't done that since her days with the foster families. Kat purred and rubbed the top of her head against the back of Birdie's hand.

"Katura," Birdie said as she began stroking the cat again. "Maybe we should go out and explore the night for monsters."

But Birdie didn't move from her chair, and after a few minutes she picked up the pen and began to write about Galiena again.

Chapter 4

At church the next morning Aunt Joyce's friends smiled, patted Birdie, and said how glad they were to have her there. Some of them remembered her mother.

"So you're Barbara's girl," they said, then peered at her even more closely. Birdie assumed her best polite face and let their pity flow past her without letting it touch her.

Still, in spite of those bad moments, Birdie didn't feel the two hours were wasted. She had plenty of opportunity to watch all kinds of people, and she was introduced to several girls her age. Tara had a pixie face and brown eyes. Becky wore braces that somehow made her cuter, and Rita kept her eyebrows slightly raised all the time as though she were waiting for the answer to a question she'd just asked. They'd all smiled, looked at her curiously, and then dismissed her when she didn't attempt to join their group.

Birdie kept an eye out for Jobee Riggs, but he wasn't there.

After lunch, Uncle Albert offered to drive Birdie to the sanctuary.

"If it's okay with you, I'll just walk," Birdie said, trying hard to remember the rules of proper family behavior. "It's not too far, is it? And I walked everywhere in the city."

Uncle Albert, relieved that his Sunday afternoon wasn't going to be spoiled after all, said that no, it wasn't far, especially if she cut through the field. After she changed back into her jeans, he went to the back door with her and pointed out the direction.

"The llama's in that field, isn't she?" Birdie asked.

Uncle Albert laughed a little. "Has Cleo been giving you trouble?" He didn't wait for Birdie to answer. "You just talk nice to her, and she won't bother you."

"What are nice words in llama language?" Birdie asked, but Uncle Albert only chuckled again as he went back to his chair in front of the television set. On the screen, a baseball player was waving his bat tauntingly, like a cat flicking his tail before pouncing on a mouse. Aunt Joyce had gone into the bedroom for her Sunday afternoon "lie down." There was nothing for Birdie to do but set out across the field as if she didn't know there was such a thing as a spitting llama. She wished she had a baseball bat.

The sheep all raised their heads at practically the same time to look at her before they dropped their mouths back to the grass. The llama, too, raised her head from the grass to stare at Birdie. Then, still chewing, the animal started across the field toward Birdie.

Birdie calculated it would take her at least six minutes to reach the fence if she ran flat out. The llama could move much faster than that, and even if it

43

couldn't, Birdie wasn't going to run from a goofy-looking, long-necked, long-legged sheep. Instead she waited till the llama got closer and used her sweetest voice to say, "Nice llama. Pretty Cleopatra. What a nice name, Cleopatra. Fits you perfectly."

The llama, altogether too close now, regarded Birdie with haughty eyes as if to say, "Cut the flattery. What are you doing in my kingdom without my permission?"

Birdie moved steadily toward the fence. "Now, Cleo, since we're going to have to share this place for a little while, we might as well try not to be enemies. I mean, I'm willing to be nice. Looks like you could try a little, too. Nice Cleo."

Birdie kept her eyes on the llama as she climbed the woven wire fence. She had one foot on one side and one foot on the other when she saw the haughty stare of the llama change to an evil glint. Birdie hastily swung her leg over the fence, lost her balance, and fell as she tried to jump. Cleopatra's projected missile of spit barely missed her.

"You no-good, four-legged, ugly beast," Birdie said in the same sweet voice she'd been using. Cleopatra lifted her chin and turned away as if the game was over for now and she knew without a doubt she had won again.

"I ought to come back in there and pop you right between the eyes," Birdie shouted, all the sweetness gone out of her voice. But she didn't move back toward the fence. She'd been knocked down plenty of times attacking things bigger than she was until she'd learned to find smarter ways to fight. Still, sometimes she couldn't fight at all, but had to play the game the way the enemy wanted it played.

She thought that might be the way it was with Cleopatra. No way to win. With a sigh, Birdie got up, brushed off her backside, and started across another field. Then she was out on the road, and a sign with the picture of a cardinal and a matching red arrow pointed the way to the sanctuary.

A much smaller sign at the entrance stated the name and the hours from April through October. Winter visits were allowed by appointment only.

Feeling a bit like a real Galiena again, Birdie followed the gravel road between thick trees until she came out in a clearing with a log cabin smack in the middle. A wooden bulletin board on the cabin's narrow front porch gave information about Burton Riggs's love of nature and the generous gift of Joseph Burton Riggs, Jr.

Inside, a short, bowlegged man with a gray fringe of hair around his head scowled at her and said his name was Mike Parker. His scowl only grew fiercer when she said she'd come about a job. So she stopped smiling and made solemn promises about her dependability.

After he made a few promises of his own, chiefly to fire her if she didn't do the job to suit him, he said, "You can mow Wednesday if it doesn't rain. The mower's in the shed out back."

"That sounds fine, Mr. Parker," Birdie said. Jobee might call him Mike, but then Jobee was a Riggs. "Is it all right if I look around today? See some of the animals and the birds?"

He gave her another sour look. "You'd probably get lost. I guess the boy could take you out, but you'll have to wait. He's out with a couple of families now, a whole pile of little kids." He frowned as if

45

something was hurting him. "They're probably breaking tree limbs and stealing all the rocks along the paths."

"I don't think I'd get lost."

"That's what they all say," Mr. Parker said. "But I guess you've got as much right to get lost as the rest of them. Here's a map."

Birdie glanced down at the marked trails on the map. "What kind of animals can you see in the woods?"

His face softened around the mouth and eyes, and for a minute, he looked almost happy as he counted them off on his fingers. "Squirrels, rabbits, and groundhogs. Chipmunks and opossums. Skunks and foxes. A few minks and weasels. Raccoons. All kinds." The hard lines returned around his mouth. "Not that you'll see any of them, except maybe a squirrel or two, because you won't know how to walk in the woods. Hardly anybody does anymore. They crash along the paths, talking and laughing, and then expect a deer to poke its nose out of the bushes for them to pat or something."

"Does Jobee?" When the old man gave her a blank look, she added, "Know how to walk in the woods?"

"He can do it when he wants to take the trouble, which ain't too often any more. His daddy's the one the animals can't hide from."

"I heard he takes pictures for magazines," Birdie said. "What magazines?"

The old man's frown wrinkled up his whole face and made a strange contrast to his smooth bald head. "You just naturally nosy or what?" he asked. "I

46

ain't no walking information pamphlet on the Riggs family.''

"Sorry," Birdie said as she retreated from the log cabin.

After studying the map, Birdie picked the path closest to the parking area in hopes Jobee and his family group would be returning on it. Although the path was well worn, bushes pushed in on her and rattled against her jeans in spite of her best efforts to slide past them quietly.

On the streets in the city and in school hallways, she'd learned how to blend with the crowds so no one noticed her. Even at the various places she'd lived, she'd been able to move about almost invisibly, but here the bushes grabbed at her legs and shook noisily as she made her escape. Even when she thought she was managing a section of the path without too much noise, the birds still flew out of the trees ahead of her, setting off alarms that echoed through the woods. Old Mike Parker was right. She wouldn't see any of the animals and she'd only catch the flutter of wings as the birds flew away from her.

She told herself she didn't care. She knew what rabbits and squirrels looked like. She began concentrating on what she could see.

Trees crowded in on her from every side. Cedars, oaks, and maples, and at least five kinds she couldn't name. She memorized the shape of their leaves in case Aunt Joyce had a tree book. Everywhere young saplings shot up straight and tall as they jockeyed with each other for a spot of sunlight.

She became slowly aware of the aroma of the woods. The smell of last year's leaves returning to the soil and the green smell of growth blended with

47

the musky smell of animals. She couldn't detect the slightest whiff of cigarette smoke or car exhaust, and she felt far away from the city, where people noises and smells dominated everything.

She'd given up spotting any animals when the squirrel Mike Parker had predicted she might see chattered at her overhead as it ran along the limbs, hopping from one tree to the next without hesitation.

While she was still watching him, she heard voices and knew the tour group must be coming. She moved off the path to wait for them, curious to see what Jobee Riggs had to say about the animals.

Leaning against a tree, she tried to hear his voice. The birds kept fluttering here and there, so perhaps they hadn't been fleeing from her so much as simply been continually on the move. The squirrel was gone, but a breeze moved the leaves in his wake. Behind her, the bushes rustled as though they couldn't keep quiet even when she did. And somewhere among the trees, coming closer, were people noises. A laugh, the murmuring of more than one conversation, and the whimper of a tired child. She caught the sound of Jobee's voice repeating some bit of information by rote.

She couldn't hear his words, but she made some up to fit the murmur of his voice. "This green thing is a tree. That blue thing with the wings is a bird. It eats seeds and worms. Squirrels live in the trees and eat nuts."

Birdie smiled even as she felt a little nervous at the thought of the boy spotting her. He'd know she'd tracked him down. Without really thinking about it, she decided to slip back up the path to the clearing before the group came into sight, but when she started to push herself away from the tree, a deer bounded out on the path. Birdie froze in place and watched it hold its head high and sniff the air before slowly turning to face her. It had antlers just like one of Santa's reindeer. Cocking his head, the deer gave her a considering look. It didn't look especially frightened, more wary and a bit surprised to see her there instead of back on the path with the others. After all, it wasn't as though people were strange to him. He must see them nearly every day.

Then, before she was through looking at him, the deer leaped away from the path and disappeared into the trees. Seconds later, Jobee Riggs came into sight.

Birdie wished she could disappear as easily as the deer had, but all she could do was stand there on the path and wait for the group to come closer. The kids who'd brought Mike Parker such a look of pain were being herded along by a mother, father, and grandmother. Some distance behind, a younger couple tugged along a two-year-old. Jobee Riggs looked thoroughly disgusted with the whole group, and seeing her didn't appear to make him any happier.

"Mr. Parker said I could look around," she said when he was close enough.

"Mike tell you which path to take?" Jobee asked.

"No, I guess it was luck I picked your path," she said, making it sound as though she weren't sure whether it was good luck or bad. "If it's okay, I'll just tag along with the rest of you back to the clearing."

"Do whatever you want. The tours are free anyway," he said.

The adults were smiling at her as the kids wandered

49

off the path to filch Mr. Parker's rocks and strip a leaf off a tree here and there.

"It's really nice back here," the grandmother was saying as the parents began urging the children back to the path. The couple with the toddler caught up, and when they let go of his hands, he picked up a rock and threw it with surprising accuracy straight at Jobee's leg.

Jobee flinched, then said calmly, "Rock throwing is prohibited in the park." The parents began apologizing and reprimanding the child at the same time. The boy let out a wail as they pried a second rock out of his hand. That plus the noise of the children coming reluctantly back to the path made Birdie feel more like she was on a playground than a nature reserve.

"The kid's got a good arm," she said to Jobee, who stared a hole through her before he turned and went on up the path.

When he began talking again, Birdie checked to see if his mouth was moving or if he'd simply switched on a tape recorder. "To your left are two large oak trees," he said, his voice slow and measured. "Oak trees supply much of the winter food for animals such as squirrels and chipmunks, who gather and store the acorns in the fall. These trees are over a hundred years old and could possibly live as long as three hundred more years." He paused under the trees. "If you look closely, you may be able to spot a squirrel."

When no squirrel peeked out through the leaves, Birdie tried to help out. "I saw one a while ago. He was running through the branches like it was a race course."

Jobee turned and went on up the path as the grandmother said, "How nice, dear. I'm afraid our group has been too noisy to see any of the animals. Still, I think it's good to expose children to nature, don't you?"

"Yes, of course," Birdie said politely, although she kept her eyes on Jobee's back. Even if he was pretending not to, she could tell he was listening, so she added, "I saw a deer, too. One with antlers."

"How exciting," the grandmother said as she collared the biggest boy. "Did you hear that, Davey? This girl saw a deer."

Ahead of them as if on cue, Jobee began reciting the next bit of his program. "The white-tailed deer is indigenous to this state and is the largest animal which still exists in the wild in this area of the country. Although prized by hunters as game animals, they are protected here in the sanctuary, as are all our animals, from both hunting and trapping. Deer are excellent at camouflaging themselves in the trees and bushes and are often able to stand or lie very near the trails without revealing themselves to the untrained eye."

"Your eye must be trained," the grandmother said to Birdie.

Jobee hardly paused. "There are also many reptiles who make their home here: snakes, lizards, frogs, and terrapins to mention but a few."

"Wow, snakes," the kid named Davey said, his interest finally caught. "Poisonous ones?"

"A few, but most of the snakes are harmless to humans and beneficial to the ecological balance of the wild here. That's what the sanctuary tries to main-

51

tain, a natural balance where all kinds of animals can survive and reproduce.''

As they came out into the clearing, Jobee said, ''Thank you for coming out to explore our corner of the wild kingdom here in Salyer County. I hope you leave with a new sense of the beauty and wonder of nature.'' His smile looked as practiced as his words sounded.

The families split apart to head back toward the log cabin. Jobee waited long enough to let them get ahead before he followed. He kept his eyes away from Birdie, who fell in beside him.

''Don't you like to give tours?'' she asked.

''That was my third one today. After a while I get tired of the same words over and over and this bunch was wild.''

''Sort of like baby-sitting, I guess.''

He shot his eyes over at her, but she kept her own eyes on the trees around them. After a minute, he asked, ''Did you get the job?''

''Naturally. I told Mr. Parker I was a hard worker and dependable.''

''Are you?'' Jobee's voice betrayed the hint of interest.

''Sure, for a couple of months anyway. After that, who knows where I'll be.''

''You going to get called back to Theopolis?'' Jobee was smiling now, not the practiced smile he'd used on the tour people, but a real smile that changed his face. She figured he was only halfway making fun of her. The other half was beginning to see what she'd known all along. They were meant to be friends.

She told herself she should be the one resisting the

idea of friendship, but even as she thought it, she was smiling back at him. "Maybe," she said. "A person like me is never too sure what will happen on the morrow."

"Then you might be at school tomorrow and you might not."

"I expect to be. I'll be at the middle school."

"Yeah, me, too. Eighth grade. I'm Jobee Riggs."

"Your folks own this place then?" she said as if she didn't already know.

"They used to. My father donated it to the county a few years ago. My grandfather was a little bit nuts over wildlife and trees, and so is Dad."

"And you're not?"

"Trees are trees, and the animals would just as soon people didn't come poking around bothering them."

"Mr. Parker said you know how to walk in the woods so that you can see the animals. Could you maybe show me how sometime?" Birdie, who didn't like asking for anything, hurried on when he hesitated. "I mean that's okay if you don't want to. I probably won't have much spare time anyway. In fact, I'd better be getting back now. I have chores to do."

He didn't say anything until she was several steps away. "Did you really see a deer?"

She stopped and looked back over her shoulder. "Sure. He had eight points on his antlers. I counted them."

"Then if you saw the deer, you already know how to walk in the woods. I could take lessons from you."

"Maybe." Birdie smiled and turned back toward the road. "See you, Jobee."

"As I said before, the probability factor is high."

It wasn't until she was halfway down the gravel drive that she realized she'd never told him her name. It was probably just as well. She might have slipped and said Galiena.

The rest of the way back to the farm, Birdie pretended she was Galiena and filtered everything she saw through alien eyes. She was so full of the story winding through her mind that she hardly noticed Cleopatra eyeing her as she crossed the field back to the farmhouse.

Chapter 5

Aunt Joyce insisted on going to school with Birdie the next day. At the school, the principal greeted Aunt Joyce like an old friend at the same time he inspected Birdie with more than a hint of suspicion. Aunt Joyce didn't seem to notice as she returned Mr. Wright's smile.

Once she was satisfied Birdie was in good hands, Aunt Joyce went home. By the time a schedule was worked out for Birdie, the first bell had already rung, and when Mr. Wright ushered Birdie into her civics class, thirty pairs of eyes zeroed in on her. Birdie studied the map of the United States on the back wall and heard Mr. Wright introducing her to the class through the fog of indifference she gathered around her.

He asked for a volunteer to show her to her classes, and Rita, the girl with the raised eyebrows from church, put up her hand. The principal, his mission accomplished, left the room, and the teacher, Mr. Monroe, rummaged in some shelves until he found her a book. Birdie found an empty seat in the back of the room while Mr. Monroe and the class tried to decide which page they were on. They finally settled on either thirty or thirty-one, and Mr. Monroe began lecturing again. His head tilted to the left as he talked, and his glasses kept slipping down on his nose so that he had to push them back every few words.

After a few curious glances her way, most of the class slouched back down in their seats and let Mr. Monroe lull them back to sleep with his facts and figures on the American form of government.

Birdie inspected the students around her one at a time, committing each face to memory. There had been so many schools, so many kids, that sometimes Birdie wondered why her memory bank of faces and names didn't burst like an overinflated balloon. Once for fun, she'd made a personal survey on the popularity of given names. There'd been sixteen Jennifers, a dozen Jeremys, ten Melissas, eleven Michaels, and so on. There had never been another Birdie or Avery.

She'd never heard anybody else called Jobee either, she thought as she spotted Jobee Riggs in the second row, third seat. He was looking toward the teacher with a marked lack of interest, but then even Mr. Monroe didn't appear to be too interested in what he was saying.

Birdie tuned in on his words. He wasn't saying anything she didn't already know. She'd read all about the three branches of government in the old set of encyclopedias she'd found in the trash, left behind by the previous tenants in one of their apartments. Before she'd come to Aunt Joyce's, she'd boxed up the encyclopedias and sent them with Kevin to Willie's, along with their other bits and pieces of furniture and keepsakes. Kevin had promised to keep Willie from pitching the books in the garbage.

The sound of Mr. Monroe's voice altered as he

asked a question. He waited for the answer, then was off again. His words droned on, piling one on top of the other.

When class was almost over, Birdie noticed the boy in the row next to her begin poking the cute, blonde girl in front of him with a pencil. He kept it up until the girl looked back at him. The silly face he made at her sent the girl into a spasm of giggles she only half tried to smother with a hand over her mouth. Birdie looked closer at the tall, dark-headed boy with a bored grin on his face.

He must have felt Birdie's eyes on him, because he jerked around to face Birdie and pulled another silly face. Without so much as a smile, Birdie kept staring at him as though trying to figure out exactly what he was. After a minute the boy's face darkened, and he turned away.

As it turned out, Birdie's giggle wasn't important since another giggle surfaced on the other side of the room. Without warning, Mr. Monroe grabbed a thick metal ruler and whapped it on his desk three times. "I will not have." Whap went the ruler. "This kind of disruption." Another whap. "In my classroom." A final whap that surely must have traveled up the ruler to sting his hand.

For a minute, Birdie thought the whole class was going to dissolve into giggles, and she realized the boy had intended to goad Mr. Monroe into doing just what he'd done.

When the bell rang, Rita bore this out. "That was Monroe's whapper. If he doesn't bang his desk at least two or three times a week, some of the kids feel cheated."

The boy who'd instigated the first giggle swaggered

out of the room in front of them. Birdie noticed Jobee pushing through some of the kids behind her, and for a crazy moment she thought he was trying to catch up with her. Then he pushed past her as if she didn't exist to catch up with the boy in front of them.

"Who's the boy?" Birdie asked.

"Barry Wilson." Rita half sighed, as if even his name was something special. "He's so cute. Half the girls in school are after him." Rita shot Birdie a sudden warning look.

"If that includes you, you don't have to worry about me," Birdie said. "I sort of doubt if Barry likes skinny redheads. Not many boys do."

"That wouldn't keep you from liking him."

"I don't think he's my type either."

"Then you don't know the right type," Rita said, hugging her books up against her.

"I guess not," Birdie agreed. "He was the one who made that first girl giggle."

"Yeah, Barry's always doing something to keep things interesting."

"Looks like he'd get in trouble with the teachers."

"Oh, he never gets caught. All the teachers like him."

Birdie didn't say any more as she watched Jobee Riggs walking beside Barry Wilson.

Rita noticed her watching Jobee and said, "That's Jobee Riggs."

"Are he and this Barry guy friends?"

"Sort of, I guess. Jobee's smart. Not too good-looking, but a real brain. Barry says it's like having a walking computer at his elbow. He feeds Jobee the information, and Jobee comes up with answers."

"You mean for his homework?"

58

"I don't know about homework. What I was talking about is the other things they do."

"You mean things like making Monroe whap his desk."

"Yeah," Rita said. "I've heard they're plotting something big now. Something that everybody's going to get in on."

"Sounds like fun," Birdie said without much interest. Whatever it was, she wasn't going to be part of it. She'd promised Aunt Joyce and Uncle Albert she'd stay out of trouble, and if that promise got broken it wouldn't be because of some kind of foolish prank.

Birdie was in class with most of the same kids all day, including Barry, Rita, and Jobee. She saw lots of other kids in the halls, but it seemed this group of thirty or so kids shared the same schedule.

By the time they went to their last class of the day, she knew nearly all their names. She'd figured out by the way they answered the teachers' questions which kids were at the top of the class, and she wondered if they'd be jealous if her grades were higher. Mostly she'd watched Jobee and Barry and the other boys who gravitated toward Barry every time class let out. He was a popular kid, but Birdie kept herself aloof from all of them except Jobee. She'd put herself in his path three times, but each time he acted as though she were invisible, even though she was trying to be as visible as possible.

The last class of the day was English, the subject Jobee's mother taught. Birdie's eyes went from the short, dark-headed woman over to Jobee, who sat hunched in his seat, staring at his desktop. As his mother instructed the class to answer the roll with a verb, Jobee seemed to sink in upon himself until he actually looked smaller. When it came his time to answer, he said, "Disappear."

Birdie wasn't sure whether he was wishing it for himself or his mother. Mrs. Riggs didn't seem to notice as she called out the next name. When it was his turn, Barry Wilson said laugh, and two or three girls in the room tittered as if he'd hit an automatic giggle button. Mrs. Riggs paid no attention as she looked up at Birdie.

"Avery Honaker," Mrs. Riggs called out.

"If you don't mind, Mrs. Riggs, everybody calls me Birdie," Birdie said.

"Birdie." Mrs. Riggs tried it on her tongue. "No, I don't think so. Your verb, please," she said as if the matter was settled.

"Disagree," Birdie said.

Mrs. Riggs looked up from her attendance book at Birdie. After a moment she said, "A very good verb." Then she folded up the book and launched into the day's lesson.

On the board she wrote out the verbs the students had used to answer the roll and instructed them to write a story using the action verbs. A lot of the kids groaned, but it was the first time Birdie had been interested all day.

Again, Mrs. Riggs didn't seem to notice as she said, "You have fifteen minutes before we move on to something else. This is just a little exercise for the mind." She sat back down at her desk. "You'll get points for each of the verbs you use correctly."

Birdie finished her story in ten minutes. After she turned her paper over, she sat back to watch the other students. Three, like her, were no longer writing. Jobee Riggs was one of them, but he wasn't looking around. He'd opened up a paperback book and gave every indication of being totally absorbed by the story he was reading. It was his way of disappearing.

Birdie let her eyes drift back to the front of the room, where Mrs. Riggs sat at her desk. She was running her fingers again and again around the smooth edges of some kind of wooden animal as she watched the class. When exactly fifteen minutes were up, she set the sculpture down gently and, gripping the edge of her desk, pushed herself up to face the class. Her eyes fluttered from face to face as she tried a smile here and there.

As she began to explain the structure of sentences, she seemed to grow more comfortable with the sound of her voice, and her grip on the edge of the desk relaxed. Still, an odd tension remained in the classroom that made Birdie wonder if the class was in the habit of baiting Mrs. Riggs into some kind of response the way they did Mr. Monroe.

Birdie glanced over at Jobee again, but he was hunched over staring at his English book now. He didn't plan to see anything that might happen. Birdie's eyes drifted to Barry Wilson, who looked every inch the model student as he sat up straight and watched Mrs. Riggs attentively. Still, Birdie was so sure something was going to happen that when the bell rang with no screams, giggles, or banging books, she was surprised.

Mrs. Riggs quickly gave them their homework assignment. As a few of the students groaned, Barry very politely said, "Mrs. Riggs, most of the other teachers give us class time to work on homework assignments."

She looked at him and considered his words seriously. "Then that is class work, if I'm not mistaken. Not homework at all. The exercise on page twenty-nine is homework." Unconsciously she reached over to touch the sculpture. Birdie could see now that it was some kind of cow, but the oddest-looking one she'd ever seen.

"Well, I guess you're right there," Barry said with a grin. "Homework it is, guys." He made the announcement to the rest of the class as though passing approval on her assignment.

Mrs. Riggs actually smiled at him as if he'd done her a favor, and the class filed out into the hall.

Birdie found herself directly behind Barry and his friends.

"Hey, Barry," one of them said. "You let her off pretty easy, didn't you? I mean, I think you could have gone for even or odd. She might have fallen for that."

"You have to go easy with these new teachers," Barry said. "Besides she's Riggs's mother. He'll come up with something to bring her into line, won't you, Riggs?"

"I don't know, Barry."

"Sure you will. I mean what good does it do to have a mother as a teacher if you can't convince her to let up a little on the assignments?"

Jobee shrugged and looked down at the floor.

"We're thinking up something, aren't we, Riggs? It's going to give all the teachers fits."

"What's the plan, Barry?" a kid named Tim asked.

"You'll know when the time comes. Until then you'll just have to anticipate." When Barry laughed, they all joined in.

Jobee laughed, too, even as he glanced back over his shoulder toward the room they'd just left. When he did, Birdie was right behind him, and there was no way he could pretend he hadn't seen her.

"Hi, Jobee," Birdie said. "Nice little school you've got here."

"Yeah, I guess," Jobee said as he ducked his eyes away from her and turned his head back around. Red began creeping up his neck.

"Hey, Riggs," Barry said. "You holding out on us? You didn't tell us you knew the new girl."

"I don't. Not exactly," Jobee muttered.

"She seems to know you," Barry said as he looked from Jobee to Birdie and then back again.

"That doesn't mean he knows me," Birdie said. "Lots of people no doubt know Joseph B. Riggs that he doesn't know."

Jobee looked at her with a flicker of surprise in his eyes.

"That right, Riggs?" Barry said.

"Ask her. She's the one doing the talking," Jobee said.

"People everywhere," Birdie said with a smile.

"Where are you from, new girl?" Barry asked.

"Oh, this place and that." Birdie assumed her most mysterious look before she headed on down the hall toward the locker she'd been assigned.

Barry stepped in front of her. "Wait a minute."

Birdie stopped and looked up at Barry. He was a couple of inches taller than her, and up close like this she could see his eyes were a smoky blue. Rita was right. He was cute.

He smiled, expecting to melt her with his charm.

63

"How come you didn't laugh in Monroe's class this morning?"

"I didn't see anything funny," Birdie said.

"Old Monroe is always funny, isn't he, guys?" Barry glanced around at the five or six boys around him. They laughed as if just thinking about old Monroe was funny enough.

"You're not laughing. What did you say your name was? Birdie?"

"That's right. My name's Birdie, and no, I'm not laughing."

"Why not? You one of those kids who kiss up to the teachers all the time?" Barry said. "Rule number one for any kid is that the teachers are the opposition, the enemy."

"Whatever you say," Birdie said.

"Now you're getting the idea," Barry said with a big grin. "Whatever I say. If you keep thinking like that you might even get your chance to join the crew."

"The crew?"

"The bunch. Us guys who keep things interesting around here. Everybody wants to be part of the crew, and who knows? You might just get your chance to help us out and be part of the crew, too."

"Help you out?"

"Oh, just a joke we're going to play on the teachers. Nothing real bad, but real funny. And we might let you be part of it."

Birdie looked straight at Barry. "Tell you what, Barry. When the time comes I'll weigh the probabilities of the situation carefully."

Barry looked from her back to Jobee. "She sounds

like you, Riggs. You sure you two aren't related somehow?''

''I'm sure,'' Jobee said. He was looking at her as though he wished she would disappear, or better yet had never appeared in the first place. Still, at the same time Birdie could tell she'd caught his interest, even if he'd die before he let the other guys know it.

''Look, it's been fun chatting, but I've got to run,'' Birdie said. ''I'll see you around, Barry and crew.''

Rita caught up with her before she got to her locker. ''Isn't he just too cute?''

''Who?'' Birdie said as she wrestled with the strange lock. ''Jobee?''

''You're trying to be funny,'' Rita said, her eyebrows inching up a little higher.

''I thought that's what everybody liked around here. People who tried to be funny.''

''Only when they happen to look like Barry Wilson. It's a shame all boys can't be that cute.''

''If they were, you wouldn't think they were that cute. You'd think they were average-looking.'' Birdie pulled the books she needed out of her locker. ''See you, Rita, and thanks for showing me around today. But I'd better get home before my aunt starts worrying.''

''You mean she's not picking you up?''

''No.''

''Then you should have ridden the bus.''

''I didn't know which one, and it's not all that far. Besides, I like to walk.'' Birdie slammed her locker shut and, with a wave at Rita, started for the front door. ''It'll give me a chance to look the town over.''

Seeing Brookdale didn't take Birdie long. There were two blocks of old storefronts with empty parking

65

spots all along the street. When everybody she passed smiled and spoke to her, Birdie began to see it was going to be a little bit more difficult to be invisible in Brookdale than it had been in the city.

Of course assuming a disguise was just another way of being invisible. Birdie thought about what disguise she was going to use at school. She could be cold and indifferent, or nice but reserved. She could try being funny and different, even weird. There might even be the remote possibility she could go for friendly and popular. For that to happen it would help if she could remold her looks and give herself petite features and blonde, curly hair. Bony redheads seemed to fit better in the weird disguises than the popular ones.

Besides, she didn't care whether she was popular or not. All she wanted to do was stay out of trouble and maybe, if the chance presented itself, get to know Jobee Riggs. He wasn't cute. Not in the official girls' handbook of cute anyway, but she was sure they could be great friends. Even if she did have to miss him when she left, maybe it would be worth it this one time.

They would be friends. But first she'd have to get past Barry and crew to convince Jobee it was possible.

Then, as she walked out of town along a street of impressive, dignified houses that quietly spoke of money, she thought about how Galiena would have handled Barry and crew. She could hardly wait till she had a pen and paper in front of her to write down the story.

Chapter 6

Dumbo the duck rushed to meet Birdie when she came into the yard, and fell on his beak. With a laugh, Birdie pushed him upright with her toe. The duck quacked his appreciation as he waddled along behind her up the porch steps.

Aunt Joyce didn't even notice the duck as she came out on the porch before Birdie got to the door. "Why didn't you ride the bus?" she asked.

"I didn't know which one, so I decided to walk today."

"Why, child, it's your Uncle Albert's bus. Didn't anybody tell you?"

"I don't think so, but the walk was nice. I got to see what the town looked like and spotted a few more streets where I might get another yard to mow."

"You've already got three, haven't you?" Aunt Joyce said. "I think that might be enough for now, at least until you get settled in, don't you?"

"I thought I might get one or two more," Birdie said. Then, to let Aunt Joyce know she was trying to do things the way Aunt Joyce wanted them done, she added, "But I can wait a while if you want me to."

"I think you probably should, and you should ride the bus tomorrow, don't you think? I mean that's a long walk. Anything could happen."

"Okay, if you think I should. Today I just didn't think I'd have time to find the right bus, and I forgot about Uncle Albert being one of the bus drivers. In the city I always walked everywhere. Everybody did. So I thought it'd be all right." Birdie piled word on top of word. It was hard explaining everything.

Aunt Joyce sighed, and her face relaxed a bit. "I guess I worry too much, but you're just a little girl in a strange place." Aunt Joyce put her arm around Birdie's shoulders. "Come eat some cookies and you can tell me about all the friends you made today."

"If it's okay, I'll just grab a couple of cookies and run. I'm supposed to mow Mrs. McCulley's yard today, remember?"

That night after supper and the dishes were finished, Birdie took her books up to her room. Her homework was simple, and she finished it quickly. Then, with Kat curled up on the desk beside her paper, she wrote Kevin another note. She told him about school and mowing the yards and asked him about his school.

She stared down at the words on the paper and wished she could talk to him to be sure he was okay. She didn't even have an address to send the letters she'd written. Still, Kevin made friends easily, and his teachers always liked him. He was like Willie that way. Willie with his laugh and jokes.

Birdie had liked Willie. That had been the easy part after Kevin was born and she went back to live with her mother and Willie. The hard part had been getting Willie to like her. She had tried being extra-good. She did whatever he or her mother told her, and most of the time anticipated their wants. She took care of Kevin when he cried and never asked for anything new. She searched for pencils in the halls at school and begged or stole the school paper she needed. But nothing had worked, and finally Birdie had figured it out. It was because she wasn't pretty. Willie liked pretty girls. She'd heard him say so a dozen times.

In the end, it hadn't mattered that much whether Willie liked her or not. He'd left them. Still, he hadn't forgotten about Kevin, and Kevin had never forgotten him. Now they were together, and it would be okay. Willie liked Kevin.

Birdie stroked Kat five or six times before she folded the letter to Kevin and laid it aside. She didn't have to worry about Kevin. He wouldn't forget her. She was his sister, and he'd want to hear the story she was writing for him. She got out the notebook with Galiena's story and read what she'd already written.

It was funny how sometimes she felt as though she might really be Galiena. She was so different from everybody else. Even when she was trying to fit in, she couldn't. Like Galiena, she'd have to forget her old ways and adopt new ones, at least as long as her stay here in Brookdale lasted.

Birdie turned to a fresh sheet of paper and began writing.

"Galiena wished she could use her powers, but it was better to keep them in hiding. She had to pretend to be one of them, and earth people couldn't make themselves invisible at

69

will. They couldn't transform their bodies into more desirable shapes or sizes, and they couldn't see through walls. She had used the mind control a few times, although she was careful to use only a small amount. Too much might make someone suspect her. These earth people were weak in some ways, but stubbornly strong in others. And suspicious of anything out of the ordinary. Galiena was definitely out of the ordinary. She must keep them from finding out just how much out of the ordinary.

"She had to become one of them. Go to school as they did. Pretend to believe their silly theories in math and science, when even newborns on Theopolis knew better.

"Still, this planet held its mysteries. Mysteries Galiena had to solve. Mostly they were mysteries of the humans, the way they thought, the way they acted. Oh, there were the monsters to beware of, the llama with her missiles at the ready and countless others out in the woods waiting. In time, Galiena would see them all, just as she'd seen the deer creature with the antlers. It had appeared in front of her eyes in the woods and then melted back into the trees with the same grace and ease of the elantus on Theopolis. Ever since Galiena was very small, she'd been told the spirits rode the elantus. Here there was a similar legend about the antlered deer. They were said to carry a saint through the heavens to every house bearing gifts on a holiday called Christmas.

"A strange legend, but perhaps true. Galiena almost wished she could stay here on this strange world long enough to discover the truth of the legend, but her assignment would be over long before the day the humans called Christmas."

"Long before," Birdie whispered as she closed the notebook and pushed it back into the drawer.

The sound of Birdie's voice roused Kat from her nap. The cat hopped up on the windowsill to look out at the darkness as if something was calling her. Her tail flicked back and forth, and she hardly noticed when Birdie touched her.

Birdie stared at the dark window. Her reflection stared back, softened into fuzzy lines by the glass, as though she might really fade out of sight if she tried. But Birdie wasn't in any hurry to fade away. It wasn't bad in Brookdale. She had her own room, and she had Kat.

Not that Kat was hers. Kat belonged to Aunt Joyce, but the cat had attached herself to Birdie ever since she'd been at the farm. Aunt Joyce didn't mind. She had never even once brought up Birdie's claim to be allergic to cats.

Aunt Joyce was trying so hard. She and Uncle Albert had taken Birdie in, in spite of what Mrs. Hansen must have told them about Birdie being a difficult child. That was bound to be in the social worker's records. *Avery (Birdie) Honaker, a child with difficulties. A child unable to establish proper relationships with other people.*

Birdie remembered the visits from the Mrs. Hansens of the past, and their questions and papers and power over Birdie's life.

"How do you like it at your new house?"

"The house is warm. I do my chores."

71

"Good." The social worker always smiled when she said good, even the times she said the word as though she didn't really mean it. "How about kindergarten? Have you made friends?"

"I know all the other kids' names," Birdie said.

"That's wonderful. Then you have someone to play with at recess."

"I like to swing. Only one person can sit in a swing at a time."

"That's right, Avery, and your teacher tells me you don't like to take turns, that she has to make you get out of the swing."

Then the conversation would go on as the social worker would try to wear her down with questions. Why do you do this, Avery? How do you feel about that, Avery? Don't you want to do this? Would you rather do that? And in her mind Birdie would be swinging, higher and higher in the air. She knew that if she just kept pumping, someday she'd go higher than she'd ever gone before and everything would be all right then. She'd be in a place where she belonged.

In a way it had worked. She'd gone back to be with her mother and had found a way to belong because of Kevin.

Maybe if he had come along with her to Aunt Joyce's, she could have belonged here, too. But whether she belonged or not, she was beginning to like it here on the farm more than she'd thought she would.

Except for Cleopatra, the farm animals weren't half bad, and the mowing jobs promised to pay well. The wild animal sanctuary and Jobee Riggs were bonuses.

She'd never wanted a friend before, but then she'd

never met anybody like Jobee before. She smiled a little at her fuzzy reflection in the window.

She had seen him that afternoon while she was mowing Mrs. McCulley's yard. He had even waved at her when she had waved at him. Once he'd seemed to be hesitating as he walked past the yard, as though debating whether to come talk to her. The next time she'd looked up, he was way up the street. She'd wanted to run after him, but she had pushed the lawn-mower down the other side of the yard instead.

Now she knew she'd done the right thing not trying to stop him. She needed to get him as curious about her as she was about him, and the best way to do that was to be a little mysterious.

Mysterious Avery Honaker, alias Birdie, alias Galiena. Birdie stared at her reflection in the window until it blurred even more. She was mysterious. No one knew very much about her. Sometimes she didn't think she knew very much herself.

Birdie turned away from the window and caught sight of herself in the dresser mirror, and there she was—plain Birdie Honaker with chopped-off red hair and freckles. Nothing at all mysterious-looking about her. Maybe her eyes, she told herself quickly to hold onto a bit of the illusion she'd conjured up while staring at the window. She concentrated on her eyes until she felt like she was staring at a stranger, but even then she couldn't feel very mysterious. Her eyes just looked back at her from the mirror, curious and alert. They were eyes that liked hunting answers, not hiding things. Computer eyes, just as her mother had always said.

Birdie laughed, and her computer eyes seemed to be demanding to know what was so funny. She turned back to the window, but the mysterious look was gone now, even in the soft edges of her reflection in the dark pane. She was still just plain Birdie Honaker.

It wasn't that she didn't have secrets. She had lots of secrets. Things she'd never talked to anybody about. Things she didn't even let herself think too much about. Some things were better with fuzzy edges, because when things came into focus too clearly the sharp corners could hurt.

Her father was one of the fuzzy secrets she often played with in her mind. He, of course, had been extraordinarily good-looking. He thought about her all the time, but he couldn't find her. He was in some kind of undercover work and couldn't risk blowing his cover by admitting he had a child. Sometimes she imagined he was from another planet, just as Galiena was. After he'd fallen madly in love with Birdie's beautiful mother, he'd had to return to his home planet galaxies away before he knew about Birdie. He had found out about her now, but he had no way to return. Her computer eyes were a gift from him, for he surely had eyes that searched for facts and answers.

There were times when Birdie almost believed her secret stories about her father.

But there were other secrets she didn't think about. Secrets from the times when she'd had no place. She turned quickly away from the thought. She was with Aunt Joyce and Uncle Albert right now, and even though she knew it wouldn't last, Birdie didn't think she'd carry any secrets away with her, except maybe her friendship with Jobee Riggs, and that would be a good secret.

Right now it was so secret even Jobee didn't know

74

about it. Birdie smiled at her reflection in the window and a tiny bit of the mysterious look returned.

Kat was still staring at the window as though transfixed by her own image. Birdie reached out and picked up the cat, who tried to cling to the windowsill with her claws as though she weren't ready to give up her view of the mysterious darkness beyond the window.

"I'll have to take lessons from you and Cleopatra," Birdie said as she stroked Kat. "Cats always look mysterious, and that Cleo has a way of making you think she's plotting something all the time."

Birdie held Kat up in front of her face, but Kat was sleepy now. She just blinked her eyes and purred. "Oh well," Birdie said. "Maybe Cleopatra will be a better teacher."

The next morning before she caught the school bus, Birdie slipped out to the back fence to study the llama. Cleopatra, who noticed her right away, lifted her chin and eyed Birdie. Birdie lifted her own chin and stared back at the llama at the same time she backed up a few steps to stay well out of range.

"You're so ugly, Cleopatra," Birdie said aloud. "Yet there's something almost enchanting about you." Birdie studied the llama a moment. "I think it's because you are so strange. You don't belong here with sheep and cows. You should be somewhere more exotic, and you know it, don't you?"

Cleopatra stretched her neck out toward Birdie like a long finger. Birdie was so mesmerized by the animal's large, round eyes that she didn't back up even though the distance between them was shrinking dangerously. Instead Birdie was considering how safe it would be to touch the llama's nose when Aunt Joyce yelled out the back door that the bus was coming down the hill and that Uncle Albert couldn't wait on Birdie any longer than he waited on any of the other kids.

At school that day, Birdie kept her chin high and let her eyelids droop a little to hide her computer eyes.

Rita noticed her different look when she fell in beside her as they went to lunch. "Hi, Birdie. Did you stay up late doing homework last night? You look sleepy."

Birdie opened her eyes all the way. Sleepy wasn't exactly the look she'd had in mind. As she looked over at Rita, she saw Barry and crew only a few steps behind them. "The homework wasn't bad. Other things kept me awake," Birdie said. If she couldn't look mysterious, maybe she could sound that way.

There was a laugh behind her as Barry said, "Hear that, guys? The new girl said other things kept her awake. Was that you, Riggs?"

She didn't need to see Jobee to know that he was trying to sink beneath the floor. Slowly, with chin high, she turned her head to look at Barry with her best imitation of Cleopatra's haughty stare. In fact she almost wished she were a llama so she could spit at him.

Barry met her look, then backed up a step. Smiling in what she hoped was an exotic way, Birdie turned back around to talk to Rita, as if Barry and his crew didn't even exist, but inside she felt a surge of power. She had to force herself not to look back at Barry with the llama stare again.

Rita was chattering on about the English homework

76

and Mrs. Riggs, and then about Mr. Monroe smacking his desk with his ruler again that morning.

"We're going for a new record. I heard Barry talking about it. No class has ever gotten him to hit his desk every day for a week." Rita laughed. "We're going to be the first."

"A worthy endeavor," Birdie said.

Rita gave her a funny look. "Well, fun anyway. Then, after we do that, we're going to start in on phase two of Barry's plan."

"Barry's or Jobee's?" Birdie asked as they got into line. She didn't even glance back to see if Barry and crew were close enough to hear her. She didn't care.

"Jobee just comes up with the ideas for Barry. He wouldn't know how to pull them off himself, and even if he could, he'd be too afraid of getting caught."

"Barry's not?"

"Barry knows he won't be caught." Rita looked at Birdie again. "Once you know Barry a little better, then you'll understand."

"I can't wait. I've always liked understanding things," Birdie said as though she were talking about a science project.

The rest of the day Birdie watched Barry and crew with eyes she hoped were at least a little mysterious, and she did begin to understand a few things. First off, Barry was the undisputed leader of the whole eighth grade. He was class president, captain of the football team, and leader of the student council. He didn't really have a special girlfriend, but rather a group of girls he seemed to be constantly interviewing for the position. Rita wanted to be part of that group, but wasn't.

The position of advisor to such an important student leader was not one to be taken lightly. Birdie had only to watch the other boys pass by Jobee in the hall and poke him hard on the shoulder with a comradely fist to understand what Jobee got out of the arrangement. It was not something he was likely to give up for friendship with a skinny, redheaded girl who didn't know how to fit in even when she was given a chance.

Barry gave her that chance on Wednesday morning between civics class and science.

"Hey, Honaker," he said. "Wait up. I want to talk to you."

Birdie would have kept going, but Rita grabbed her arm and made her stop. Birdie turned slowly, the llama stare at ready in case she needed it. "Yeah, Wilson. What do you want?"

She almost smiled at the look on his face. Nobody called him Wilson. He was Barry. But Birdie's very indifference as to whether he liked her or not gave her an edge.

He recovered quickly. "I'm going to give you your big chance, Honaker. Tomorrow you get to make old Monroe whap his desk."

"I thought that was your specialty," Birdie said.

"Anybody can do it. A little talking when you shouldn't. Dropping a few books. Falling asleep. It's not that difficult."

"I'm sure it isn't," Birdie said. "But Mr. Monroe's not a half-bad teacher. A bit boring, but I certainly wouldn't want to disrupt one of his lectures."

A couple of the kids around them giggled, and

Barry turned to glare at them before he looked back at Birdie. "Don't you want to be part of the crew, Honaker?"

"Not really, Wilson," Birdie said as Rita gasped beside her. "Why should I?"

"Lots of reasons. Riggs, tell Honaker some of the reasons." Barry poked Jobee's arm.

But Jobee just stared at Birdie, and then at Barry, as though he couldn't think of a thing to say.

"See," Birdie said after a few seconds. "Even your computer friend can't come up with any reasons. At least logical ones." Then she slipped into science class seconds before the late bell rang. Barry and nearly all of his crew got late slips, including Jobee. It took Mrs. Hatton ten minutes to write them all out.

Chapter 7

It didn't rain, so that afternoon, Birdie threw her books on her bed and ran back down to the kitchen to grab the sandwich Aunt Joyce had fixed for her.

"I don't know what Mrs. Hansen is going to think about these mowing jobs," Aunt Joyce said worriedly as she watched Birdie gulp down the sandwich. Aunt Joyce looked back down at the sweater in her lap. Her needles clicked, and the sweater almost magically grew as Birdie watched.

Birdie swallowed her bite of sandwich and asked, "When is she supposed to come check up on me? Or I guess it won't be Mrs. Hansen way out here. Does Brookdale have social workers?"

"I talked with a Miss Franklin to begin with. She works in this area."

"Then no doubt Miss Franklin will be the one who'll come. Is she devoted to her job?"

Aunt Joyce looked up. Her needles slowed but didn't stop as she said, "She seemed to care, if that's what you mean."

"Oh no." Birdie groaned, then laughed at the look on Aunt Joyce's face. "Don't look so upset, Aunt Joyce. It's just when they're devoted, they ask so many questions. You'll find out."

"They just want to make sure you like it here." The needles stopped, and Aunt Joyce dropped her hands in her lap. "You do like it here, don't you, Birdie?"

When Birdie didn't answer right away, Aunt Joyce rushed on. "I mean, I know you miss your mother and Kevin. That's only natural, but your uncle and I want you to be as happy as you can be while you're here."

"It's nice here, Aunt Joyce." Birdie looked down at the table as she answered. She wanted to say the right thing. "Different, but nice." She looked up at Aunt Joyce. "And don't worry about Miss Franklin. She'll think it's great that I'm mowing yards. Trust me. She'll think it's a 'positive' sign."

"You sound so cynical, Birdie. Those agency people are just trying to do what's best for you and Kevin and even your mother."

"I suppose," Birdie said quickly. "Have you heard anything from Mama? How she's doing? Or Kevin?"

"I would have told you, dear, if I had, but they said your mother would need weeks and probably several months of therapy. She's an alcoholic, you know."

"Yeah, well, lots of people are," Birdie said, her eyes drifting to the window. She could see the llama's odd head high above the woolly backs of the sheep.

"You've got to understand the pressures she's had trying to raise you and Kevin without very much help." Aunt Joyce seemed to be explaining it to herself as much as to Birdie.

Birdie wanted to say that she had helped, but she kept quiet. Grown-ups never thought kids knew how

81

to help, and maybe she hadn't known how. They'd been split apart. Birdie brushed that thought aside. "Do you think maybe we could try to call Kevin sometime?" she asked. "You know, just to be sure he's settled in and everything."

"I think that's a wonderful idea, Birdie. We'll try to get his number and do that this weekend." Aunt Joyce picked up her needles and began knitting again. "Maybe if we can work things out, his father will let Kevin come here for a visit after a while. I'd love to see him again, and he'd like the animals. Don't you think he would?"

"He'd like the animals," Birdie said, and then, because Aunt Joyce was trying so hard, she dropped a kiss on her cheek before she went out the back door. "I don't know when I'll be back. Mr. Parker didn't tell me how long it takes to mow," she called back before she let the door close behind her.

When she got to the sanctuary, Mr. Parker was waiting with detailed instructions. She did everything exactly as he said. By the time she was finished, the frown was easing back on his forehead, and when she slipped and called him M.P., he almost seemed to like it.

Jobee was there, too. Mr. Parker told her the boy was out clearing some of the trails, but although Birdie caught sight of Jobee a couple of times while she was mowing, she didn't try to talk to him.

It was late when she finished, so she headed back to the farm as soon as she'd put the mower away. She could too easily imagine Aunt Joyce standing by the front door, worrying.

It was a funny feeling having somebody worry about her. It felt sort of like she was wearing a coat a couple of sizes too small, and Birdie wasn't sure she liked it much.

She was almost to the end of the gravel road when she heard something behind her. She turned slowly in case it was an animal, but it was only Jobee on his bike.

"Oh, I thought you'd gone home a long time ago," Birdie said when he caught up with her.

Jobee slid off his bike beside her. "Nope. Mike had some last minute things for me to do at the cabin."

"I thought you only worked on the weekends."

"I work when Mike needs me to." Jobee studied her a minute, as if he were trying to see something he'd missed before. Finally he went on. "Mike was really impressed with you. Said you were a good worker."

"Yeah, old M.P.'s okay."

"M.P.?"

"Don't you think it fits? Mr. Parker didn't seem to mind," Birdie said as she started walking again. "I've got to get on back. My aunt worries when I'm late."

Pushing his bike along, Jobee fell in beside her.

Birdie looked over at him. "You don't have to walk with me. I can take care of myself."

"You don't want me to walk with you?"

"I don't care one way or the other, but you could get home faster if you rode."

"Probably, but my mother won't be worried about me. She'll be so busy grading homework papers, she won't even notice I'm not there yet. She's really into this teaching thing."

"She's a good teacher. Different. I like her."

"You've got to be kidding." Jobee looked over at Birdie. "Most of the kids think she's weird."

"Why? Because she shows them run is an action verb by running down the aisles between their seats?"

"That's one good reason." Jobee stared down at the ground and made a face. "She just doesn't do things like they expect. Like the other teachers."

"So? Maybe that's good."

"That's easy for you to say. You're not her kid," Jobee said. "If she'd just leave that stupid cow at home."

"You mean the wooden sculpture she likes to hold?"

"That's the one. She calls it her lucky cow." Jobee made another face. "Dad bought it years ago when he first began taking pictures, before Lori and I were born."

"Who's Lori?"

"My big sister. Anyway, he wasn't sure the magazine was going to buy his pictures, and he and Mom were over in this foreign country somewhere and almost all their money was gone. So he bought this cow. To make a long story short, the next day he heard that the magazine was going to buy his photos and an advance was on the way. So he and my mother decided the cow must be a lucky charm. Now Mom thinks it'll help her the same way. Make her a success as a teacher, you know." Jobee glanced over at Birdie and quickly away. "I told you she was sort of weird."

"I like her," Birdie said again.

They walked on a little way, his bicycle tires rolling on the road the only sound between them. After a few minutes, Birdie went on. "And who knows?

Maybe the cow will work. I mean, it must have worked for your father. My aunt says he's famous."

"But the cow didn't have anything to do with it. He takes good pictures."

"I'd like to see some of them," Birdie said.

"We've got magazines all over the place at home and one whole room of blowups. Maybe you can come over some time and look at them." Jobee didn't look at her.

"Sure, why not? Maybe the next time I mow Mrs. McCulley's yard, I'll come on up that way."

Again the rolling bicycle tires made the only sound as they walked on. This time Jobee broke their silence. "What's your father do?"

"I think he's in intelligence work," Birdie said.

Jobee jerked his head around to look at her. "You mean he works for the CIA?"

"Not exactly. More like the TSPA."

"I've never heard of anything like that."

"Of course not. It's the Theopolis Scientific Probe Agency. No one on earth would know about it."

"You're weirder than my mother," Jobee said, but he was smiling a little.

"That's just the point," Birdie said quickly. "Are you entirely convinced that there can be no aliens undercover here on earth studying the habits of the people? I mean, entirely convinced."

"Anything's possible, but the probabilities are slight."

"What you mean is that the probabilities of us knowing about it are slight. And who knows? If aliens have ever come to earth, they might have mated with earth humans and left behind children. I

85

could be one of those children. As you have already so kindly pointed out, I'm weird enough.''

Jobee laughed out loud.

''You think it's funny,'' Birdie said without cracking a smile. ''But can you say it isn't possible?'' She stared at him, letting her eyes practically click as she concentrated on details of his appearance: the scratch on his ear, the smudge on his glasses, the sweat streak on his forehead. ''Note my computer eyes. Do normal earth people have computer eyes?''

''Barry says I talk like a computer sometimes, and I'm normal.''

''Are you?''

''Close enough, I guess. If I could ever grow a few inches taller,'' Jobee said. ''But we're talking about you. Tell me more about your father from Theopolis.''

Birdie assumed her most mysterious look as she gazed up toward the sky. The sun had gone down, and the blue of the sky was deepening, ready to drift into night. Already one of the stars had begun to shine. ''There's not a lot I can tell. My mother fell desperately in love with him, and then he forbade her to ever talk about him to anyone, even me.''

''But she must have, since you found out about him.''

''She didn't tell me. I inherited some of my father's mind power along with my computer eyes. There are some things I just know.''

''You're funny, Birdie,'' Jobee said. ''I think maybe you've been reading too much sci-fi.''

''They don't have science fiction on Theopolis. They deal strictly in facts, proven facts.''

''And where is this Theopolis?'' Jobee asked.

86

"Oh, out there somewhere." Birdie made a sweeping motion at the sky and then stopped to stare as another star appeared.

"That one?"

"No, that's too close."

"I just wondered. You seemed awfully interested in it."

Birdie began walking again, still looking up at the sky. "Don't you like stars, Jobee?"

"I guess everybody likes stars, although actually our image of them is nothing like they really are."

"I know, but I'm not used to seeing so many stars. In the city, there are too many lights, but out here it's different."

"I guess your schools were a lot different, too."

"Not so much. Bigger, but not so different," Birdie said. She could see the fence she should climb to cut across the field, but she kept walking along the road with Jobee. She didn't especially want to cross Cleopatra's field in the near-dark anyway.

"Maybe they're more different than you think," Jobee was saying. "In a school like Brookdale's, everybody knows everybody. In fact, we get to knowing each other so well we can sort of guess what the other guy is going to do."

"Gets sort of boring sometimes, doesn't it?"

"I don't know. It makes it easier for guys like me who like to figure the probabilities of things happening." Jobee glanced over at her and then concentrated on keeping the wheels of his bike exactly straight as he pushed it down the road. "How come you turned down your chance to get in good with Barry?"

"I guess I didn't care whether I was in good with him or not," Birdie said slowly. "At least not enough to chance crossing one of the teachers. I don't expect to be here long, but while I am here, I've promised my aunt and uncle I'll stay out of trouble."

"Your aunt and uncle real strict or something?" Jobee asked.

"No, just real nice," Birdie said. Up ahead she could see the farm, and while she didn't really want to stop talking to Jobee, she knew Aunt Joyce would be peeking anxiously out the window watching for her. Birdie went on. "Besides, being part of Barry and crew just isn't on my list of must-dos."

"Why not?" Jobee asked. "Most of the girls think he's cute. Take Rita, for instance. She'd probably dance on old Monroe's desk if Barry asked her to."

"Maybe so, but I'm not Rita."

"If Barry likes you, then other people at school will, too."

"You don't understand, Jobee. I don't care whether people like me or not."

"You want me to like you," Jobee said with a sideways glance toward her.

Birdie shrugged a little as she stopped at the end of the driveway. "It was just an idea. The other day when I saw you playing basketball, I thought you looked intelligent. I thought maybe we could talk."

"About Theopolis?"

"Sure, why not? It's a pretty interesting place."

"I told Barry you were weird, and that this wasn't going to help," Jobee said.

"What wasn't going to help?" A stillness grew inside her. "Did he tell you to talk to me?" She didn't wait for Jobee to answer. "Do you ever do anything he doesn't tell you to do, Riggs?"

"I don't know why you're getting mad. It's a good

probability I would have talked to you anyway this afternoon. It's just that to Barry you represent some kind of challenge. He wants you in the crew.''

"He's using you, Jobee. Can't you see that?" Birdie forced her voice out calm and cold. "He says 'Riggs, do this' and 'Riggs, do that', and Riggs does.''

"I don't do anything I don't want to do.''

"He's using you," Birdie repeated flatly.

"You think I don't know that? I mean, like you said, I am intelligent. In fact, I test highest levels in everything.''

"Testing smart and acting smart are two distinctly different things." Birdie turned away from him. "Look, I've got to go in. I promised my aunt I'd get home before dark.''

Jobee grabbed her arm. "I don't know why I'm telling you this. I don't care what you think, but did you ever consider the fact that maybe I'm using Barry as much as he's using me?''

Birdie turned and faced Jobee's glare. "What do you mean?''

"Aren't you smart enough to figure that out?" Jobee propped his bike against the gatepost and faced her squarely. "I mean, look at me. I'm not very tall. I have to wear these awful glasses all the time or I can't see." Jobee yanked off his glasses and shook them at her. "And my nose is too big.''

"There's nothing wrong with your nose.''

"If there's nothing wrong with my nose, then my face is too small." Jobee put his glasses back on slowly. "Something doesn't fit right anyway. And on top of all that I'm just too smart. All through grade school I never had any real friends, so when I got to

89

middle school I decided I was going to change things. I'm the one who made Barry see how he could use me. He'd have never thought of it on his own.''

"I guess it worked out good for you. You're part of the crew.''

"That's right,'' Jobee said. "And I'm not going to mess up all my hard work getting where I am today just because of some weird girl who plans to disappear back to Theopolis any time now.''

"Probably not for a couple of months,'' Birdie put in.

"But I'm not leaving in two months, and I plan to use Barry and crew right on through high school. It feels good having somebody to hang around with in the halls. I like being called Riggs.''

"If that's all you want, I can call you Riggs.''

"You don't understand.'' Jobee stared down at the ground.

"Yes, I do,'' Birdie said. "And it's okay. Really. Like you said, I won't be here long, and I am a bit strange. Who knows? Maybe we'll have a couple of chances to talk down at the sanctuary before my spaceship comes to pick me up. None of Barry's crew would have to know.''

"Why don't you just try to fit in at school? It's not hard to make old Monroe whap his desk. Just about anything will trigger him.''

"And if I do that, what will Barry decide I should do next?'' Birdie shook her head. "No, I don't mind being a loner.''

"I think you're just afraid of a little trouble.'' Scorn filled Jobee's voice.

"And I think you don't know what you're talking about, Jobee Riggs, but I pick my own trouble. I don't let someone else pick it for me. Just you remember that.'' Without another word, Birdie turned and ran up the lane toward the house.

Halfway there, she looked back over her shoulder to see him riding away on his bike. As she slowed to a walk, a heavy feeling settled inside her that had nothing to do with being tired. It was beginning to look as though Galiena was going to have to go solo in figuring out the mysteries of this strange world after all.

Chapter 8

The next morning, Barry stepped in front of her as she was going into civics class. "Riggs says you haven't changed your mind about getting old Monroe to whap his desk this morning, but then Riggs isn't always right." Barry glanced over at Jobee, who was staring off down the hall. He gave no sign of hearing anything Barry was saying.

"I'm sure he's right more times than most," Birdie said sweetly. She kept her eyes away from Jobee completely.

"He gets too caught up in facts sometimes. Me, I know how to read people better, and I say you've changed your mind," Barry said, his eyes back on Birdie. "After all, it's your big chance to show you're one of us."

"I guess it is," Birdie agreed.

"Good. I'm glad we understand one another."

"One of us understands one of us anyway." As she went on into the classroom, she smiled a little at Jobee without appearing to look at him at all. He knew though, even if no one else noticed. Birdie was sure of it, and she almost forgave him for letting Barry use him.

After all, what difference did it make to her if he hid behind a disguise at school? Wasn't she always wearing some kind of disguise herself? The invisible girl. The good girl. The girl from another world. The rebel. Whatever disguise fit the time and place.

Behind her she could hear Barry. "See, Riggs. I told you she'd come around. You've just got to know how to talk to girls." He changed the tone of his voice to match Jobee's. "And the probabilities are that I know more about that than you do."

Around him the crew laughed. Jobee laughed, too, and in front of them Birdie's mouth twisted in a half-smile. The smile disappeared as she took her seat and adopted the guise of the perfect, conscientious student.

As the minutes of the class ticked by, Birdie could feel Barry looking at her, but she didn't allow her eyes to slide over to meet his until the class was half over.

He was cute, as Rita said at least three times between every class, but when Birdie pulled each feature out individually, she had no trouble spotting a few imperfections. He had a fuzzy spot in his hair right above the left ear. His eyes were almost too small, although they were a nice blue. Not as nice a blue as Jobee's, but she was studying Barry now.

In her mind she divided out categories and began to fill in the slots. A couple of eyebrow hairs drooped down from his eyebrows as if they didn't want to belong with the rest. A zit was turning red on his chin, and if anybody's nose was too big, it was Barry's. She stared unblinking at his nose for a full minute. There was something comical about even the best-shaped noses.

Barry's eyes narrowed, and he jerked around to face the front of the room. Birdie kept staring at the side of his face until the red had climbed up from his neck into his cheeks. Then she calmly focused her attention back on Mr. Monroe. After a few minutes of concentrating on the teacher's words, she looked around at Jobee. He was watching her, just as she'd known he would be.

Birdie smiled at him, and he quickly turned away from her to open and close his book a few times. Then, almost as if it were an accident, he pushed the book off his desk. It slammed flat against the tile floor. Two or three students followed Jobee's suit, and before the last book hit the floor, Mr. Monroe had his ruler in his hand and was whapping his desk.

Birdie felt Barry's eyes on her again, but she kept looking at Mr. Monroe as though he were still lecturing on the subject of the Supreme Court instead of raging about young people's inability to pay attention.

At lunch, Rita laughed about Mr. Monroe's class and took pains to explain to Birdie how easy it was to get Mr. Monroe upset. The more she talked, the surer Birdie was that Barry had instructed Rita to bring her into the camp, just as he had sent Jobee to talk to her the night before.

As she listened to Rita, Birdie let her eyes drift over to Barry, who sat on the other side of the cafeteria surrounded by his crew. Barry sat in the middle. Jobee was on his right and Tim was on his left. Scott, Will, Jamie, and David, who made up the rest of the core of the group, were on either side and across the table. Girls were mixed here and there among the fringes of the group.

Birdie imagined sitting at that table, belonging to

a group. She'd never belonged to a group, even the fringe of a group. At most of the schools she'd attended, she'd been only a faint shadow in the halls, and it had been easy to fade out completely. But here at Brookdale, it was different. Instead of fading out of sight, Birdie stuck out so much that she was always bumping into something or somebody.

Over at that other table, Jobee said something, and the rest of the table waited until Barry laughed before they joined in.

Birdie turned her eyes back to Rita, who would have loved to be at Barry's table. Perhaps she hoped to gain entrance to Barry's inner circle by getting Birdie to cooperate with Barry's plans.

"There's just one thing I want to know," Birdie finally said as they gathered up their trays to carry them to the window. "Why does Barry want me to do it?"

"What difference does that make?" Rita said. "It's all for fun."

"He can get Monroe to whap his desk without my help. Jobee did it for him this morning."

Rita looked at her for a minute before she answered, "Think of it as a kind of initiation. A test of sorts."

"A test?"

"To see if you've got the courage to be in with the rest of the crew."

"And what was your test, Rita?" Birdie looked at her closely. When she didn't answer right away, Birdie went on. "Maybe getting me to take the test is your test. You're not in the crew, but you want to be. Me, I don't care. The big question is, why does Barry care?"

Rita frowned at her. "Maybe the question is why you don't."

"You want the truth, Rita?" Birdie looked over at her as they made their way through the hall.

"Jobee told Barry you wouldn't know how to tell the truth if your life depended on it," Rita said.

"Jobee said that?"

Rita backed off a little. "Well, something like that anyway."

Birdie laughed. "And how about Jobee? Does he always tell the truth, the absolute truth?"

"I've never really thought about it, but I guess he does," Rita said. "He's never been in any trouble that I know of."

"Never? No trouble at all?" Birdie didn't wait for her to answer. "That's pretty amazing."

"Why do you say that?"

"I thought you had to get into trouble to be part of Barry's crew."

"Getting Monroe to whap his desk is not getting into trouble. He's been teaching for years, and I don't think he's ever even sent anybody to the office. He just lectures."

"I knew he was a great guy," Birdie said as she got her books out of her locker.

Rita leaned against the locker next to Birdie's and waited for her. Birdie thought if she didn't watch herself she might get used to having somebody to hang around with in the halls, and Rita wasn't half-bad. She knew lots of things about the other kids that made them more than just names and faces.

"Then you'll do it," Rita finally said as they started toward their next class.

"If I say I will, you still wouldn't know whether

to believe me or not, would you? I could be lying, since the truth is so hard for me.''

"You know, you're sort of strange sometimes," Rita said with the beginnings of a frown.

"A strange bird?" Birdie grinned. "A cuckoo bird? A bird of another feather?"

"A funny bird at any rate." Rita's frown was replaced by a smile. "But I sort of like you in spite of it, even though I don't think I understand you. I mean, if Barry likes you, everybody will like you."

"That's what Jobee said, but tell me. What if Barry doesn't like me? What happens then?"

"I don't know." Rita shrugged a little. "But you don't have to worry about that, because all you have to do is get Monroe to whap his desk and you're in."

"What am I in? And why am I in? I don't like questions without answers."

"You sound like Jobee, always wanting to know all the answers." Rita's eyes narrowed on her, and her eyebrows came down as if she'd finally gotten an answer to one of her own questions. "That's why you're always wanting to talk about Jobee, isn't it? You two are alike."

"In some ways," Birdie said as the bell rang. "In others, we differ greatly. You see, he wants truthful answers, and I take any answers I find."

Birdie spent the rest of the day dividing her attention between the teachers and Barry Wilson. Even if his nose was a little funny-looking, she couldn't deny he was cute. All the other kids liked him. Why was it that she couldn't just fall in step behind him, too?

That's what the social workers had kept telling her when she was with those other families. "Just try,

97

Avery. Just try to do things the way your foster parents want you to do things.''

The funny part then was that she had been trying, not because she wanted to stay with them, but because she didn't want trouble. She'd wanted to be invisible. She'd wanted to go into a kind of frozen sleep until she finally found somewhere to belong.

Birdie smiled to herself as she changed classes. Could it be that here at Brookdale Middle School she'd found a place she could belong, and now she didn't want to? But she already had a place to belong.

She belonged with her mother and Kevin. She'd been taking care of them. She could have kept taking care of them if Mrs. Hansen hadn't butted in. Of course, that was Birdie's fault. She shouldn't have skipped so much school.

Wherever she went, whatever happened, somehow it was always Birdie's fault, but it wasn't going to be her fault here. She was going to give even the hint of trouble a wide berth.

To do that, she planned to study Aunt Joyce and Uncle Albert until she figured out what they expected from her. She was going to learn about the farm animals and try to spot some of the wild animals at the sanctuary, because she wouldn't have much chance for that kind of thing when she went back to the city. And she was going to make Jobee into a friend. If not at school, at least they could be afterschool friends. That was a lot to do in a couple of months or less. She just didn't have time to play Barry's games of harassing the teachers.

In the last class of the day, Mrs. Riggs rubbed her lucky cow and had them diagram sentences on the blackboard. Everybody else groaned, but Birdie volunteered to go first. Jobee's mother so wanted them to learn that Birdie didn't think it polite to refuse.

After the last bell rang, Birdie rushed to her locker and then for her bus. Since that first day, Uncle Albert watched for her, and if she was late, it held up all the buses behind him.

She was almost to the door when Barry stepped in front of her. "What's your hurry, Honaker?"

"I've got to catch my bus." Birdie tried to slide past him, but the rest of the crew closed ranks around her. Birdie looked for Jobee, but he was off to the side, leaning against the lockers. She tried, but she couldn't read the look on his face. She looked back at Barry. "All right, Wilson. Make it quick."

"Rita tells me you want a second chance."

"Yeah, sure. That's me. Second Chance Honaker."

"Good. I'm glad you're beginning to see things my way. Once the bit with Monroe is on the record books, then we're going for something more exciting. We'll drive them crazy."

"What's that? Are you going to write nasty words on their chalkboards?"

"Maybe. If we do, they'll be there awhile. Right, Riggs?" Barry looked to his right, and his smile disappeared. "Where's Riggs?"

"Don't panic! He hasn't deserted the ranks. He's right over there." Birdie pointed. "And I've got to go. It's been nice chatting with you." She pushed through Tim and Scott. "Excuse me, guys."

"You've got just one more chance, Honaker," Barry called after her.

"I'll keep that in mind," Birdie said over her shoulder as she went out the door. Again she looked at Jobee, and this time she recognized the look on his face. He'd closed down his computer eyes. He wasn't gathering or processing any new information. He was just standing there wishing he were somewhere else, or that she was. Maybe on Theopolis.

Birdie ran down the steps toward the line of buses. About the only chance she had of ever getting Jobee to talk to her again was another Barry order.

The bus was rolling, and Uncle Albert was shutting the door when she reached it. He smiled at her in relief. "I didn't think you were going to make it today," he said.

"Neither did I," Birdie said. "Thanks for waiting."

At the farm, Aunt Joyce looked up from her needles and wool to smile at Birdie. "There's a snack on the table."

Birdie looked at the plate of cookies. "You don't have to stop knitting to fix me cookies, Aunt Joyce."

"I need a break every once in a while anyway," Aunt Joyce said. "Are you in a rush? Do you have a yard to mow?"

"Not today," Birdie said as she nibbled on one of the cookies. "Where's Kat? She didn't come meet me at the door."

Aunt Joyce looked up and around. "That's right. I let her out at lunchtime, and she hasn't come back in. Oh dear." A touch of dismay flashed across Aunt Joyce's face.

The cookie in Birdie's mouth became pieces of gravel that she couldn't swallow. "You think she's hurt?" she managed to ask. Birdie thought of all the things that might have happened to the cat, and she felt not only a little sick, but mad at herself as well.

She should have never started to like the stupid cat in the first place.

Aunt Joyce laughed a little. "No, I don't think that's the problem. I think she's feeling romantic. Cats have a way of doing that when the seasons change. I guess I'll end up with more kittens."

"Oh," Birdie said.

"I should have her spayed, but I like kittens, don't you?"

"Sure, why not?" Birdie started chewing her cookie again. "The more animals the merrier."

Still, later when she was up in her room, Birdie missed Kat sitting in the window or on the desk beside her.

"Dumb cat," she muttered as she pulled out the notebook with Galiena's story in it. She didn't need friends, animal or otherwise. She picked up her pen and began writing.

"Galiena's plans to recruit a human guide to show her the mysteries of this strange planet had failed. Even Katura had deserted her. She was alone to face the monsters of the planet, and there were many."

When Birdie paused to think, her hand itched to reach out and touch Kat. She scrubbed it hard against the edge of the desk and started writing again.

"Galiena wasn't afraid. She'd faced monsters on other planets. She'd face these, and soon she'd learn what she needed to learn so that she could return to Theopolis. Maybe it was for the best that Katura had deserted her. She would have had to leave her behind when she left. Galiena knew the rules. And she knew her mission. She must accomplish it before she could return home.''

''Birdie,'' Aunt Joyce called up the steps. ''Can you come down a minute?''

Birdie gripped her pen and thought about visits from Mrs. Hansen or Brookdale's Miss Franklin. More monsters for Galiena to face. She called back as she stood up, ''What's going on?''

''Come see. Kat's brought a friend home with her.''

Birdie shoved the notebook in the drawer and ran down the steps two at a time.

''They're out on the back porch,'' Aunt Joyce said.

Meowing, Kat streaked across the porch to rub against Birdie's legs, while the big yellow tom stayed aloof even when Dumbo the duck began quacking at him.

''We'll have to find out whose cat this is,'' Aunt Joyce was saying behind her.

''I know,'' Birdie said. ''His name's Ralph, and he belongs to Jobee Riggs.''

Chapter 9

The big cat lazily draped his front paws and head over her arm as she carried him toward Jobee's house. Aunt Joyce had offered to drive her, but there were the animals to feed and supper to start.

"Maybe if you just take him down to the road, he'll go on home by himself," Aunt Joyce had suggested.

"He might," Birdie agreed, but then, when she got to the end of the drive, she hadn't given Ralph the chance. She'd carried him on toward Jobee's house even though the big cat was getting heavy.

Just as she'd hoped, Jobee was shooting baskets out behind the house. She stalked straight across the concrete court, dodged the basketball when it bounded off the rim, and dumped the cat in front of Jobee. Ralph landed lightly on his feet in spite of his bulk and shook himself a little.

"Yours, I believe," Birdie said. Then, without another word, she turned to leave.

"What are you doing with Ralph?" Jobee asked.

"Ask him," Birdie said without slowing down. "Or maybe you don't need to ask. Aren't you the one with all the answers already?"

"I thought that was you," he yelled at her back.

Birdie slowed down long enough to smile over her shoulder at him. "Maybe so. But you can't believe my answers, can you?"

She was nearly to Mrs. McCulley's house before Jobee caught up with her. "I had to put Ralph in the house," he said, panting a little. "How come you left so fast?"

"I figured that's the way you wanted it," Birdie said. "I thought you didn't want to be seen talking to an outsider like me."

"I never said that." When Birdie looked at him, he went on. "Not exactly in those words anyway."

Birdie turned her face away so he couldn't see the smile threatening to turn up the corners of her mouth. Maybe Galiena wasn't going to have to be a complete loner after all. As she walked on without saying anything, Jobee fell in beside her.

"You still haven't told me what you were doing with Ralph," he said.

"What do you think?"

"I think the probabilities are that your aunt has a female cat. Ralph is an amorous Romeo."

"You're very good with your probabilities."

"I know." Jobee stopped walking, took off his glasses, and rubbed the lenses off on the bottom of his T-shirt.

Birdie stopped, too. They were in front of Mrs. McCulley's yard now. "That's a pretty yard," she said. "I wonder if Mrs. McCulley would care if I put up a sign that said "Lawn Maintenance by Honaker.' "

"You'd most likely have to offer her a cut rate." Jobee put his glasses back on without re-attaching the safety strap. It flopped around behind his ear as he considered the yard carefully. "Not that many people see Mrs. McCulley's yard except the neighbors here on the street, and you've already approached most of them about mowing. I'd say you'd get at the most one job out of such an advertisement and that you'd be better off charging her the full rate and hoping for an increase in business through word of mouth. Mrs. McCulley likes to talk. If she's pleased with your work, she'll tell everybody she sees."

Birdie stared at Jobee, then grinned. "Is that the kind of answer you give Barry when he asks your opinion of a plan?"

"No. I keep it much simpler."

Birdie laughed, and after a minute, Jobee smiled along with her. "Don't you like Barry? I mean, really," Birdie asked.

"Sure I do. Barry's a nice enough guy. If you weren't so determined to be some kind of loner, you might think so, too. In fact, you'd probably be stuck on him like all the other girls." Jobee's face changed. "Come to think of it, that could be your problem now."

"My problem?" Birdie said.

Jobee's smile was gone as he studied her. "You like Barry, but you don't think he'll like you. So you pretend not to like him."

"And what good is that going to do me?" Birdie asked.

"I don't know. Save your pride maybe."

"The probability is that you're one hundred percent wrong, Mr. Riggs."

"Oh well, even computers can come up with the wrong answers if they don't have all the correct facts." Jobee turned away from her and began walking again. "What are the facts?"

"Facts?"

"About you. Why do you want to be an outsider?"

"Things are simpler that way," Birdie said. "Besides, my mother says I like to be different. She used to say that if someone told me the sky was blue, I'd say it was purple just for the sake of argument."

Jobee looked up. "The sky is blue."

Birdie looked up, too. "Actually, although the sky may look blue here, on Theopolis it is purple, and when the sun comes up, the sunrises are a beautiful, glowing green."

"Sounds awful," Jobee said, but he grinned. "I've got an idea. Why don't you come on back to the house and shoot some baskets?"

Birdie's insides leaped up at the thought, but she remembered Aunt Joyce. "I can't. My aunt's expecting me back."

"You could call from my house and ask her if it was okay."

"Is that what you're supposed to do when you're going to be late?"

Jobee gave her a funny look. "Sometimes you sound like you really are from Theopolis."

"Maybe I am," Birdie said as they turned back toward Jobee's house.

When they went in the back door, Mrs. Riggs glanced up from a stack of papers on the table. "Avery, how nice to see you," she said. "Jobee told me you lived close by."

With an awkward smile, Birdie searched for something polite to say in response. Then she saw it didn't matter, for Jobee's mother had already turned her attention back to her pile of papers.

Jobee raised his eyebrows over the rim of his glasses and shook his head a bit at Birdie as he said, "Birdie wants to use the phone."

Mrs. Riggs murmured something without looking up, and Jobee pointed Birdie toward the next room, even though she'd spotted a phone on the kitchen wall.

"We'll use the phone in the family room," he said. He led the way down a hall and into a comfortably untidy room of overstuffed couches and pillows grouped in front of a large-screen television. On the walls, pictures of exotic animals were mixed in with photographs of people of all nationalities. Eyes waited for Birdie every way she looked. A shot of Jobee when he was much younger shared the place of honor over the longest couch with a photograph of a pretty girl who looked about thirteen or fourteen. Magazines were stacked high on the tables and piled higher on the floor beside the couches.

Birdie looked back at the picture of the pretty girl beside Jobee's. Blonde, blue-eyed, she smiled out of the picture with the same easy confidence that Barry Wilson had.

"Who's she?" Birdie asked.

"My sister, Lori."

"She's pretty."

"I know. I just don't understand why. My mother and I, well, you know what we look like, and while Dad's not bad-looking or anything, he's not exactly handsome either. I think maybe they found Lori on the doorstep."

"Your eyes are the same as hers," Birdie said.

"Don't tell her that. She'd schedule plastic surgery tomorrow."

"I'll bet she thinks you're cute. I've got a little brother, and I think he's cute."

"You don't know Lori. She's Miss Popularity of Brookdale High. She tries to forget the fact that she's got a weird brother."

"You're popular. You're part of the crew."

"As Barry's personal computer," Jobee said.

"I thought that's the way you wanted it."

"Not exactly, but it's better than walking around the halls alone, as you're sure to find out for yourself."

"I'll survive." Birdie turned her eyes away from the picture of his sister to the one of Jobee. In it he looked like he might be a little older than Kevin. He was already wearing the dark-rimmed glasses, but they didn't hide the intense concentration in his eyes as he got ready to shoot a basketball. His dark hair was sticking to his forehead, and sweat dribbled down his face.

"I hate that picture," Jobee said.

"I think you're cute." Birdie grinned.

Flushing, Jobee looked away. "Are you going to call your aunt or not?"

After Aunt Joyce gave Birdie permission to stay, they went out to Jobee's court, where Birdie taught him a few moves, compliments of Harry from the city. They didn't keep score playing one on one, but after she beat him in two straight games of horse, he listened when she showed him how to improve his shooting form.

Just before she left, Jobee said, "Basketball must be a popular sport on Theopolis."

"You might say that." Birdie whipped the ball hard toward him. "See you tomorrow, but don't worry. I won't embarrass you by trying to talk to you."

Jobee caught the ball and held it on his hip. "I told Barry you weren't going to do it. He still thinks you are, you know."

"I know." Birdie smiled a little. "But I'm sure someone else will step in to save his plan from failure. Maybe Rita. Maybe you."

Later, back at the farm, Birdie went with Uncle Albert to feed the calves and the outside cats at the barn. On the way back to the house, she passed by the llama, who was watching her across the fence. Uncle Albert was still at the barn checking something about his tractor.

When Birdie stopped well out of spitting range directly in front of Cleopatra, the llama drooped her ears and reached out her head toward Birdie. Her eyes radiated meekness.

"Are you trying to make friends, Cleo?" Birdie said softly as she stepped near enough to touch the llama's head. Cleopatra let her stroke her nose for maybe three seconds before she whipped back her head and spat. Birdie jumped back, but not quite quick enough or far enough.

"You're a real sweetheart, Cleo," Birdie said as she brushed at the llama's saliva on her arm. "And I'm a real jerk for falling for that old trick."

Then Birdie laughed, surprising herself and Cleopatra as well, if the way the llama jerked back her head was any indication.

"Did she get you?" Uncle Albert said behind Birdie.

"Yeah, but that's okay. That's just her way of making sure I remember that she's different and not just one of the sheep."

Uncle Albert laughed. "She's one of a kind all right. At least around here."

"Does she ever spit at you?" Birdie asked.

"She did when we first got her, but I acted like it didn't bother me, and after a while we worked out a friendly agreement. I treat her like a queen, and she lets me feed her."

"Are all llamas like her?" Birdie asked as they went on toward the house.

"I hope not for the sake of those people down in South America. They have whole herds of them."

Birdie laughed as she went in the back door ahead of him. Aunt Joyce was on the telephone. When she hung up she looked first at Uncle Albert and then at Birdie with such a solemn face that their smiles disappeared at once. "That was Miss Franklin, Birdie," Aunt Joyce said. "She says she'll come by next week."

"It's routine, Aunt Joyce. Nothing to worry about," Birdie said.

Aunt Joyce sighed. "I guess so, but they sound so official or something. I'm always afraid I'll say the wrong thing."

"You don't have to say anything special." Birdie hesitated a moment before she went on. "Did she say anything about Kevin?"

"I asked about both your mother and Kevin. She said your mother was 'progressing,' but she thought it best if we didn't contact her yet. Miss Franklin says your mother will write to you when she's a little further along in her treatment."

110

"And Kevin?"

"She promised to bring his address when she came. She said she'd get in touch with Mrs. Hansen back in the city to find out about him, but that she was sure Kevin was doing fine." Aunt Joyce stopped and tried a smile. Then, as if she were trying to convince herself, she added, "She sounded real nice."

"They're all nice," Birdie said. "I've got to wash up. Cleopatra got me again."

"Oh dear, do you think maybe we should get rid of Cleopatra?" Aunt Joyce said.

"Nobody else would take her." Birdie tried to make a joke, but Aunt Joyce looked so worried that she went on. "It'll be okay, Aunt Joyce. Miss Franklin doesn't have to know that Cleopatra likes to spit at me."

In the bathroom Birdie scrubbed her arm hard with a soapy washrag until her skin was red. As she slopped on some of Aunt Joyce's lotion to hide the last lingering traces of odor, she wondered if Miss Franklin would be like Mrs. Hansen.

If so, Aunt Joyce wouldn't have to worry about Cleopatra. Mrs. Hansen would be glad the llama had spit at her, but Birdie wouldn't tell Aunt Joyce that for fear her aunt might repeat it to the social worker who came, and the dreaded words "improper attitude" would be written down on her report.

Birdie stared at herself in the mirror over the sink. Her eyes darkened. Of course, it wasn't going to last. In another couple of months she'd be back in the city with her mother and Kevin, and things would be the way they were before. Maybe even better if her mother was able to get a job.

111

Still, she was going to miss the farm and Aunt Joyce and Uncle Albert and even Brookdale Middle School, with all its exciting daily events such as Monroe whapping his desk and Mrs. Riggs stroking her lucky cow. Of course, she'd rather be with Kevin, because Kevin needed her.

Nobody needed her here except maybe Jobee, and he didn't know he did. He thought he had everything planned perfectly already, and Birdie was more in the way than anything else. But they had had fun playing ball. He was beginning to like her in spite of himself.

A warm feeling crept through her and settled in her middle like Kat curling up in her lap. She stared at her face in the mirror as she tried to figure out the feeling. It was good. She liked it, but it was also strange.

Then she knew. The anxious feeling that sometimes grabbed at her throat back in the city when there wasn't much food in the refrigerator or when she couldn't rouse her mother off the couch to go to bed had disappeared. Here she didn't have to worry about what they were going to eat or whether her mother had enough money to pay the rent.

She missed Kevin, but there was nothing she could do about their being apart until their mother was better.

"Supper's ready," Aunt Joyce called down the hall, all the nervousness gone from her voice.

It might not last forever, but it would last long enough. Aunt Joyce wouldn't send her away for no reason, and the social worker would be able to see the security of this house. Birdie could quit worrying about institutions or foster homes. The warm feeling inside her seemed to start rumbling just like Kat purring.

Then, because the feeling was so strange and she wasn't sure she should trust it, she leaned up close to the mirror and whispered a warning to herself. "Don't get too happy. You can't be *sure* it will last long enough."

Chapter 10

The feeling was still curled up inside her, purring softly, when she went to school the next day. In civics, Mr. Monroe gave a pop quiz. As Birdie concentrated on getting every answer correct, she pretended not to notice the other kids peeking over at her while the silence grew in the room. Barry even poked her once with his pencil, but she ignored that, too.

They were handing in their tests with only minutes left before the bell when Rita jumped up from her desk suddenly and, with a little help from the boy behind her, it fell over with a resounding clatter. Enough giggles followed to bring out Mr. Monroe's ruler.

After the bell rang, Barry told Birdie, "You won't get a chance to be part of any other plan, Honaker."

Birdie smiled at him. "Good." She kept her eyes away from Jobee. After all, she'd given her word not to embarrass him.

At lunch Birdie sat alone. Flushed with the success of her morning, Rita had found a place at Barry and crew's table. As Birdie ate her hamburger, she thought of the case studies Galiena could write about these humans and their strange customs.

Nobody bothered Birdie in the halls, and she had no problem at all catching her bus that afternoon.

That was the way she wanted it, Birdie told herself as she mowed the yard at the farm that afternoon. Kat, who seemed content with her adventure of the day before, lay curled in the sunshine on the porch, not even moving when Reever flopped down beside her. Dumbo the duck followed Birdie as she pushed the mower around the yard. The duck waddled along faster and faster in an effort to keep up until he finally toppled over on his beak.

After Birdie righted the hapless duck, her eyes caught the llama who stood pressed against the fence, neck stretched out toward Birdie. Birdie smiled as she began pushing the mower again. She fit right in here at the farm. This was a place for different things. An ugly cat with a misshapen ear, an off-balance duck, and a mysterious, spit-happy llama.

When she was almost finished mowing, she looked up and spotted Jobee at the edge of the yard. She pushed the mower over the last bit of unmown grass before cutting off the motor.

"Hello, Jobee Riggs," Birdie said as the animals all raised their heads to look at him. Out in the field the llama began to sway her head back and forth as though contemplating a new target.

"Is it safe to come in the yard?" Jobee asked from the gate.

"You mean because of the animals?" Birdie asked and then went on. "They're basically harmless, except the goat likes to butt your legs sometimes and the llama out in the field can't be trusted." She pushed the mower over to the gate to meet him. "What are you doing here?"

115

"I've been to the sanctuary, and old Mike wanted me to ask you if you could come work tomorrow."

"That grass won't need mowing until next week."

"No. He thought maybe you'd want to do some other kinds of jobs besides mowing, and I said you probably would."

"What kinds?"

"He wants you to go around with me so that when we get real busy later in the fall you can help out with some of the tours."

"I've got to mow a yard in the morning."

"You can come in the afternoon." Jobee hesitated before he added, "That is, if you want the job."

"Sure, I want it. But I don't know much about animals."

"Looks like you've got them all over the place around here."

"Not wild animals."

"I'll teach you what you need to say, and if you don't know the answers to the crazy questions people ask, you can either fake it or tell them to ask Mike. They won't stump him, because he'd make up an answer before he'd admit he didn't know."

With a slight shrug, Birdie smiled. "Then why not? It sounds interesting."

"Not really so interesting after a while, and you have to be nice to everybody no matter what."

"I can be nice."

He looked at her a moment before he said, "I guess we'll find out."

Birdie laughed. "You sound like you don't think it's possible, but I'm being nice at school. That's why Barry has put me on his list."

"I don't want to talk about Barry with you. While

116

I don't understand why you couldn't drop your book or giggle so old Monroe would whap his desk, that's your problem." Jobee straightened his glasses. "At the same time, I can't say I really understand Barry making such a big deal over it either."

"He's not used to people going against his decrees, no doubt especially girls who are supposed to faint and fall over at the sight of him. Have you ever noticed how funny-looking his nose is?"

"I don't want to talk about his nose or anything else about him. If we're going to work together at the sanctuary, that's got to be rule number one."

"Sure," Birdie agreed easily. "You got a lot more rules?"

"Not yet, but I may think of some." Jobee shoved his hands in his pockets and looked down at the ground. "I guess that's all I wanted. See you tomorrow then." He turned to go.

"Wait up, Jobee," Birdie said. When he stopped, she rushed on. "I mean if you're not in a big hurry or something, we could get a drink and then I could show you around the farm."

"I wouldn't mind getting a closer look at the llama." Jobee looked out toward the field, where Cleopatra was leaning over the fence, her ears pointed toward them as if she were tuning in on every word.

"I wouldn't get too close a look if I were you," Birdie said as she led the way to the house.

Aunt Joyce fussed over them and brought out cookies even though it wasn't long until supper time. Kat twirled her body around first Birdie's legs, then Jobee's, as she purred loudly. When they went back outside, Dumbo tried to follow them off the porch and fell on his beak. Reever looked up at Jobee with sad eyes, and Maybelle tried to grab a mouthful of his jeans.

Cleopatra eyed them as Birdie and Jobee approached the fence. Birdie hung back, but Jobee kept getting closer and closer as he recited information about llamas in general. "They're extremely useful animals. Not only is their wool valuable, but they make excellent pack animals even in difficult terrain. They can go for weeks without drinking water, you know. They get adequate moisture from green plants."

"I'd say that was according to how much spitting they do," Birdie said.

Jobee smiled over his shoulder at her. "Yes, that is one of their defense measures. Also, if you load them down too heavily, they'll lie down and refuse to move. My father has used them for pack animals on several of his assignments, and he says they're strange but interesting animals."

"I can't imagine Cleopatra packing anything for anybody." Birdie stopped well away from the fence and warned him. "If I were you I wouldn't go too close."

"Why not? She looks friendly enough," Jobee said. "My father says animals instinctively know when you mean them no harm."

"But are you sure you know when they mean you no harm?" Birdie asked as Cleopatra raised her head. The llama's eyes glittered with purpose, and at the last second, Birdie yanked Jobee out of the way of the llama's foul missile. As they tumbled to the ground, the llama wagged her head and her lips twitched up and down over her teeth.

"It looks like it's laughing." Jobee sounded so

118

astounded that Birdie couldn't hide her own laugh. After a minute, Jobee smiled a bit self-consciously as he added, "I guess I'd better listen to you when it comes to this particular animal."

Later, when Jobee started home, Birdie walked with him down to the road. "Why are you here, Birdie?" he asked suddenly.

"What do you mean why am I here? My parents met, fell madly in love, and here I am, the visible result of that love."

"That's not what I meant, and you know it," Jobee said. "I meant why are you here living with your aunt?"

"My mother's sick, and Aunt Joyce is doing her duty for her sister's child. Not that she acts like she minds," Birdie added quickly. "And I've already told you about my father and how he had to go back to Theopolis."

Jobee stopped at the end of the driveway and looked at Birdie. "You know, the more I'm around you the easier it is to believe the crazy things you say. So I guess I'll see you tomorrow if some space-ship doesn't come for you first."

"It probably won't. I figure I've got at least another month here, maybe even two."

She stood at the end of the drive and watched him until he was almost out of sight before she ran back to the house. She couldn't wait till supper was over so she could pull out her Galiena notebook and write a new installment: "Galiena and human friend face the monster llama."

The next day at the sanctuary, Jobee showed her the trails and recited some of his set speeches about the animals. He promised to teach her to walk quietly in the woods when they had more time. Between tours, they laughed over the crazy questions the visitors asked and decided that someday they would write a book of silly answers for stupid questions.

By the time she got home late that afternoon and saw the bicycle Uncle Albert had pulled out of the back of the garage and fixed up for her, Birdie was beginning to wonder if any of it was really happening. Maybe she was still back in the city or on the plane headed to a new place, and all this was simply an elaborate fantasy she was making up.

But when she took the bike for a trial run down the drive and let the wheel wobble so much she fell over, the pain of her scraped knee was real. Tiny bubbles of blood seeped out of the skin on her knee, but instead of crying, she smiled as she looked at it. The purring of the good feeling inside her was so loud she could barely hear the voice warning her that it wouldn't last.

The only thing that tugged at her happiness as she got back on the bicycle and rode it to the house was the thought of Kevin. If only he had come here with her.

The following days were more of the same. She and Jobee never spoke at school, but as soon as school was over they got together to shoot baskets or explore the sanctuary. At the farm, they ate Aunt Joyce's cookies while devising stratagems to teach Cleo some manners, and at Jobee's house, they leafed through magazines looking at his father's work.

After confiding in her that he liked taking nature shots at the sanctuary, Jobee showed her some of his own pictures. Birdie told him a little about the story she was writing about Galiena, but when he asked to read it, she said she'd promised her little brother he could read it first.

Actually she hadn't. She hadn't talked to Kevin at all. Aunt Joyce had tried to find a number to call him on Sunday, but there were almost a dozen William Bakers listed for the city.

So the afternoon she came home and saw the strange car in the driveway that she instinctively knew belonged to the child welfare worker assigned to her case, Birdie was almost glad. Answering a few questions was a small price to pay for news of Kevin.

Aunt Joyce and Miss Franklin were discussing the best color for sweaters when Birdie went in. Miss Franklin's folder and pen were laid aside as she sipped a cup of coffee and ate brownies that were still warm from the oven. The living room was spotless, and Aunt Joyce was wearing the dress she'd worn to church the Sunday before.

Miss Franklin set down her cup and smiled at Birdie. "And this must be Birdie," she said. "Or perhaps you'd prefer Avery."

"No, Birdie's fine. I'm used to it." Birdie smiled, too. They were always happier if she tried to act happy, and as Birdie kept smiling, she realized she wasn't having to do that much acting.

As soon as Aunt Joyce left the two of them alone, Miss Franklin eased into her questions. None of them were hard to answer, even the ones about school.

"The classes are easy," Birdie said. "I think I'm doing okay."

"How about friends?" Miss Franklin asked. "A girl your age needs friends."

"I've met lots of nice kids at school. I've gotten to know a few of them pretty well."

"Then you've made friends. That's wonderful."
Miss Franklin made a notation on one of her papers.
"I'm sure you've found the school to be a lot differ-
ent from the one you attended before."

"Different, but interesting," Birdie said. Actually
school hadn't been as bad this week as she'd expected
after bucking Barry and his crew. None of them
talked to her, but she'd discovered others who
weren't part of the crew. A girl named Jana had
started sitting with Birdie at lunch, and then there
was Howard, who had the locker next to Birdie's.
He liked to punch her on the shoulder and tell her
the latest stupid joke. She didn't always laugh, but
Howard didn't seem to care. He just kept coming
back with new jokes.

So refusing to be part of Barry's crew hadn't turned
her into the complete outcast Jobee had predicted it
would. The worst thing about it was that she couldn't
talk to Jobee at school.

Now Birdie turned her attention back to Miss
Franklin, who was still talking about the advantages
of smaller schools. When she paused for breath,
Birdie asked about Kevin.

Miss Franklin shuffled through some of her papers
before she answered. "There's not much I can tell
you. You understand that Mrs. Hansen will be the
one talking to him, not me. However, I did bring
your brother's address and telephone number. I've
already given that information to your aunt."

"Then it won't be breaking any rules if I call
him?"

Miss Franklin smiled. "We don't have that many
rules, Birdie. We just want what's best for both you

and Kevin, and Mrs. Hansen and I agree the two of you should maintain contact during this separation.''

''That means I can call him if Aunt Joyce says it's okay?''

''Yes.'' Miss Franklin smiled and then hesitated as if waiting for Birdie to say something more. After a moment, she went on. ''Don't you want to know about your mother?''

''You told Aunt Joyce on the phone that we couldn't talk to her yet.''

''Perhaps not talk to her, but we can certainly pass on news about her to you.'' Miss Franklin's voice was gentle.

''How is she then?'' Birdie asked stiffly, because she was expected to.

''She's progressing well in the treatment program.'' Miss Franklin studied Birdie for a moment. ''You mustn't be bitter because of your mother's illness, Birdie. You do realize that alcoholism is a disease, don't you?''

''I know it's not my mother's fault,'' Birdie said softly. She knew whose fault it was that they had all been separated. The thought made her feel guilty for the fun she'd been having with Jobee the past few days.

''It's no one's fault, Birdie. Not really.'' A frown spoiled the smooth lines of Miss Franklin's face. ''Perhaps you'd like me to set up some counseling sessions so that you could better understand your mother's illness.''

Birdie kept the sigh inside her and chose her words carefully. ''That might be helpful, but I'm not sure I have the time. I'm staying pretty busy helping Aunt

123

Joyce and Uncle Albert with the animals here on the farm, and then keeping my yards mowed."

Miss Franklin's smile returned. "Yes, your aunt told me about your mowing jobs. I think that's wonderful, and you really seem to be adjusting well to Brookdale. I know Mrs. Hansen will be pleased when she sees my report."

Later up in her room, Birdie wrote in her Galiena notebook.

"Galiena's heart slowed to a normal, steady thump-thump. The local planet authority had just concluded her probing questions. Routine, she said, but Galiena knew she could never think of anything as routine while she was here on this strange planet. In spite of the way her heart had pounded, she must have given the right answers, for the authority had smiled as she left. The kind couple, who had taken Galiena in even though they worried about her strangeness, was relieved.

"That was all to the good, for although she had gathered many facts, there were still more things to learn about this place. The llama monster had yet to be tamed, and there were others to be found and studied in the wilds. She needed more time, and she had bought it with her answers. Her disguise had fooled them completely. It could be she might even chance communication with Theopolis the next full moon."

When Birdie put down her pen and sat back, Kat jumped down from the desk into her lap. Birdie rubbed the cat's head absentmindedly.

The interview with Miss Franklin had gone much better than Birdie had expected. They'd gotten Kevin's phone number and had tried to call after supper, but there was no answer. Aunt Joyce had promised they would try again the next day.

Kat purred and arched her back against Birdie's hand. The only touchy moment in the interview had been when she'd failed to ask about her mother as Miss Franklin had expected her to.

It was easier for Birdie not to think about her mother. That way she didn't have to remember how angry her mother had been after Mrs. Hansen had left the apartment that first day. Now Birdie couldn't quite shut out the memory of her mother yelling and Kevin crying and nice old Mr. Winston from the apartment upstairs knocking on the door to see if everything was all right.

As Birdie stroked Kat over and over until static electricity crackled and snapped along the cat's back, she thought all that seemed so far away here on the farm, where Aunt Joyce and Uncle Albert never raised their voices except to call the animals to feed.

The peace of the farm made it easy not to think about what might happen when her mother was better. Still, Birdie couldn't shake the feeling that things were never going to be the way they had been before. Sometimes she wondered if she'd ever even see her mother again. She might just vanish from Birdie's life the same way Birdie's father had.

Chapter 11

The next night Kevin's voice sounded small and faraway over the phone. Birdie wondered how she sounded to him as she asked him how he was getting along.

"It's nice here, Birdie. Daddy's rented a real house and I have my own TV in my room. Daddy lets me watch cartoons whenever I want."

"You shouldn't spend all your time watching television, Kevin," Birdie said. "I mean you don't want to forget to practice your reading, and you need to go outside to play ball sometimes."

"I am, Birdie. I'm in the bluebird reading group at school, and Mrs. Jamison draws smiley faces on my papers all the time," Kevin said proudly. "And Daddy's been playing ball with me. He says you taught me to shoot real good."

Birdie couldn't keep from smiling at Kevin's recital, while at the same time she felt curiously let down. She hadn't exactly wanted him to be unhappy, but she had expected him to miss her. "That's great, Kevin," Birdie said now. "Everything's pretty nice here, too."

"Do you have a television?"

"Not in my room, but there's a big one in the living room."

"Good," Kevin said.

"I'll write and tell you all about Aunt Joyce's farm," Birdie went on. "She's got the funniest bunch of animals, and I'm writing you a story about them and a girl from outer space. I'll read it to you when we see each other."

"When will that be, Birdie?" His voice suddenly sounded shaky, and Birdie could almost see him with the big receiver pressed close against his small, round face and the tears filling up his dark brown eyes.

Her own eyes felt a little damp as she answered, "Not so long, Kevin." She went on quickly before he could ask how long that was. "And I'm glad you like it there with Willie. I'll write to you, and then you can send me some of those papers with smiley faces or maybe draw me a picture."

After that, as the days passed, Birdie watched for things she could write about in her letters to Kevin. She wrote to him about how Cleopatra would blink her eyes and twitch her ears, as if inviting Birdie to come closer so that the llama could spit at her. She remembered the best of Howard's jokes to pass along to Kevin, and she described the wild animals she spotted at the sanctuary.

True to his promise, Jobee had taught her to walk silently in the woods. The two of them had begun keeping a list of the animals they spotted and diligently wrote out descriptions as though they were field scientists. Jobee had taken some pictures of her when she led her first tour at the sanctuary, and she'd mailed one of them to Kevin. Kevin, in turn, sent her drawings and his school papers with rows of carefully formed cursive letters.

Miss Franklin made another visit to the farm and told Birdie she could write to her mother. Birdie wrote the letters dutifully, but she was always glad when the letter was long enough to fold and stuff in the envelope.

So the month of September passed, and with the first frost of October the trees at the sanctuary began turning brilliant hues of red, yellow, and pink. Birdie's yards no longer needed mowing as often, and she spent more time at the sanctuary conducting tours or exploring the paths through the woods, often alone since Jobee no longer came to the sanctuary on weekdays. To his great excitement, he had made the basketball team and had to practice every day.

Still, Birdie was at his house or he was at the farm so much that Birdie was sure Jobee realized now that they were meant to be friends. They thought alike in some ways and totally differently in others, but ideas seemed to spark between them as they brainstormed solutions to first one problem, then another.

They came up with an idea for a map dispenser for the sanctuary. Mike Parker laughed at them, but he let them build it. They tried to design a device to keep Dumbo the duck from falling on his beak, but so far hadn't come up with anything practical.

However, most of their time was spent planning inventions to make space travel feasible. They told each other that was so Birdie could someday get to Theopolis to see her father, and there were times when both of them believed it.

Yet in spite of their growing friendship, Jobee still ignored her at school. Birdie tried not to let it bother

128

her. She'd promised Jobee she wouldn't interfere with his plan for popularity, but the more she thought about it, the sillier it seemed. If Barry really liked Jobee, he wouldn't stop just because Jobee spoke to Birdie.

At least she didn't think he would. She wasn't too sure what Barry Wilson might do. After the week of getting Mr. Monroe to whap his desk, he had organized a plan to mix up the books on the library shelves. Miss Harrison, the librarian, had eventually ended up in the principal's office claiming persecution by unknown students. Dire announcements were made over the intercom, but that didn't slow Barry down. A few days later half the math class did the wrong assignment three days in a row, until even the teacher was no longer sure what she'd assigned for the day. Yet Barry always managed to look so innocent.

Birdie took to studying him cooly in odd moments during their classes. She truly wanted to see some good qualities about him, so that she could believe Jobee was right to want to be his friend.

As for Barry, he acted as if Birdie didn't exist. His crew had orders to act the same, so Rita told her one day at church.

"It's nothing to do with you, Birdie. I like you. Really I do," Rita said, looking more than a little uncomfortable. "But Barry just gets these ideas, and when he does there's no changing his mind. I mean I told him you were a nice girl and since you were new, you just hadn't understood about old Monroe, but he said he'd given you more chances than most girls."

"Don't worry about it, Rita. Barry doesn't bother

129

me," Birdie said with a smile. "And I know you wanted to be part of the crew before I showed up on the scene."

"Yeah, well, sometimes I wonder. I mean Miss Harrison has always been so nice, and she had a lot of trouble putting all those books back in order."

"But wasn't it fun?"

"I don't know. It was supposed to be," Rita said.

"Was it Jobee's idea?" Birdie asked casually.

"I guess so, but I don't really know that either."

Neither did Birdie. She sometimes came close to asking Jobee, but she always stopped herself. They didn't talk about Barry. It was rule number one in their friendship. Besides, it didn't make any difference to her what went on at school, as long as she wasn't part of it. All she needed to do was stay out of trouble, and she was managing that. Her grades had never been higher, and she actually enjoyed most of her classes as long as Barry didn't have some plot afoot to undermine the teacher.

Now Birdie looked at Rita and asked, "What's next?"

Rita sighed. "I'm not sure, but Barry says it'll drive all the teachers crazy, not just one of them."

"Sounds exciting," Birdie said.

The next Monday Birdie watched the crew. Barry himself rarely ever did any of the dirty work. He just set his, or maybe Jobee's, plans into motion. On her way out of civics, she noticed Tim and Scott sidling up by the blackboard to slip a couple of erasers under their shirts.

By the end of the week, the teachers were beginning to notice the scarcity of erasers, and on Friday, all the teachers began their classes with lectures ex-

130

cept, of course, Mrs. Riggs. She was much too involved with the book reports they were giving orally to notice how many erasers were on her chalkboard tray.

Birdie decided the only thing Mrs. Riggs might miss was her cow sculpture, which she still touched often for confidence. Every time she did, Jobee sank a little lower in his desk.

All that weekend at the sanctuary Jobee seemed to have his mind on other things. Even talking about her new idea for growing foodstuffs on their spaceship didn't pull him out of his somber mood. Usually he was quick to go into the details of why or why not one of Birdie's ideas would work.

Birdie finally gave up and just talked to M.P. between the tours. Birdie liked M.P. in spite of his crankiness, and she had sort of an unstated goal to make him smile at least once a weekend. Although Jobee laughed at her and said M.P. wanted friends about as much as Cleopatra, Birdie just went on thinking up things that might make the old man's face settle into one of his rare smiles.

On Sunday, probably because she spent so much time talking to him, she got him to smile twice, a feat she pointed out to Jobee as they rode their bikes toward home after the gates to the sanctuary closed.

"Mike's just playing a game with you, Birdie. Haven't you figured that out yet? He's not nearly as cross as he acts. Half the time he's smiling under his frown," Jobee said impatiently.

Birdie slowed down and fell a few bike lengths behind as she thought about what Jobee said. Then she pedaled hard to catch up. "You know, I believe you're right, Jobee."

"I'm always right," Jobee said shortly, his eyes still on the road in front of him.

Birdie pedaled along beside him without saying anything for a few minutes. Then she finally asked, "What's wrong with you this weekend, Jobee? You worried about something?"

"Why should I be worried about anything?" Jobee said without looking at her.

"It's the ball game, isn't it?" Birdie said. The first basketball game was on Tuesday night. "You're afraid you won't do well."

"I probably won't even get to play." Jobee was quiet for a minute before he went on. "My dad's coming home for the game, you know."

"That's great. Where is he now?"

"Mexico, or maybe Brazil. I forget."

That sounded as far away as Theopolis to Birdie, and she felt a flash of envy as she thought about Jobee's father coming all that way to see him play ball.

Jobee didn't seem to notice as he went on. "I wish he wouldn't. I'm not going to get to start. You know I won't."

"That doesn't mean you won't get to play."

"Getting in the game doesn't mean I'll do any good."

"You'll do okay. If it'll make you feel better, I could come over and practice with you a while before supper."

"Sure, why not?" But he didn't sound any happier.

"Something else is bothering you," Birdie said after a while.

"Yeah? What makes you think that?" Jobee glanced over at her, then quickly away. After a mi-

132

nute, he went on. "Okay, it's these crazy erasers. The other things we could get away with, but we're not going to get away with this. I know we're not. Somebody is going to get into trouble."

"All you have to do is make sure it's not you," Birdie said. "I haven't seen you taking any of the erasers anyway."

"I took a couple out of math class."

"Really? I didn't see you."

"Of course you didn't. I didn't aim for anybody to see me."

Birdie hesitated and then pushed the question out fast before she could change her mind again. "Was it your idea, Jobee? All this with the erasers, I mean."

"Partly," he admitted. "But I thought we could just take a few, enough to be bothersome but not enough to stir up a storm. Barry's getting carried away by the power he has over the crew."

"None of you has to do what he says."

"I know. I've been thinking a lot about it lately, but most of the things we've done haven't been that bad."

"Tell that to Miss Harrison," Birdie said.

"I guess that was pretty mean."

"What would you do if he did something like that to your mother?"

They had come to a slight hill they usually had no trouble riding up, but today Jobee slipped off his bike and began walking. Birdie put on her brakes and got off her bike, too.

"I'm not sure Mom would even notice, but I have thought about it." Jobee looked over at Birdie as he balanced his bike with one hand and straightened his

133

glasses with the other one. "I can't say I like having Mom as a teacher. Still, she is my mother."

"And she is trying extra hard to be a good teacher," Birdie put in softly.

"I know. I'm glad she didn't notice the erasers. If she'd just leave that stupid cow at home."

As they approached the top of the hill, Jobee slowed down even more. Birdie said, "Maybe you can talk to Barry. You could get him to believe it'll be fun to start putting the erasers back."

"I doubt it," Jobee said. They were at the top of the hill. "But I don't guess it does any good to worry about it now. I'd be better off worrying about hitting my shot if I get a chance to shoot in the game Tuesday." He jumped on his bike. "Come on. I'll race you back to my house. You can call your Aunt Joyce from there."

An hour later they were so intent on their basketball game that neither of them noticed Barry Wilson come around the house until he spoke. "What's going on, Riggs?"

Jobee's face, red already from the exertion of their game, turned even redder as he stared at Barry as though his eyes were playing tricks on him. He took his glasses off, rubbed them on his shirt, and put them back on. Finally he said, "Hello, Barry. What are you doing here?"

"I just came by so we could talk about the plans for tomorrow. I want everything to go right." He glanced over at Birdie. "What's she doing here?"

Birdie, who had grabbed the last rebound, still held the ball. Now she bounced it on the concrete as she answered before Jobee could. "I live down the road, and I was just helping Jobee on his head fake before the game Tuesday. I knew this really great basketball player back in the city, and he taught me lots of moves.''

"Head fakes, eh?" Barry said. "Some kind of fake anyway. The two of you looked pretty friendly, if you ask me.''

"You don't have to be friends with someone to play ball with them,'' Jobee said quickly.

Birdie's heart began thumping funny inside her. She kept her eyes away from Jobee as she said softly, "I guess that's true enough.'' She dropped the basketball and watched it bounce away from her, each bounce shorter until the ball was just rolling on the concrete as it passed Jobee's feet. He didn't move to stop it, and the ball kept rolling until it hit the grass next to the court.

Birdie waited another few seconds, half hoping Jobee would take back his words, admit they were friends no matter what Barry Wilson thought, but the silence beat against her ears. She used her most casual tone to say, "Well, see you around, Riggs, Wilson.''

All the way around the house to where she'd left her bike, she kept thinking Jobee would come after her and apologize, but he didn't. She didn't let herself look back until she started pedaling down the circular drive. There was no sign of Jobee. He'd had to make his choice and he'd made it.

She blinked hard to keep back tears, and the fact that she wanted to cry made her madder than ever. She thought hard about the story she'd write in Galiena's notebook when she got home. Galiena had let herself get too fond of her human friend. She had to keep her mission in mind. Maybe they'd be exploring for secrets, and the human, due to his inferior abilities, would fall off a cliff or get trampled by the monster llama.

Birdie shook her head at the thought. She didn't want Jobee to be hurt, even in her story. Maybe the best and easiest thing would be for Galiena to simply return to Theopolis.

Birdie looked up at the sky where the first stars were beginning to shine. Maybe the spaceship would come now, and she wouldn't have to go back to Aunt Joyce's and smile and eat her supper as if nothing was wrong.

Birdie slowed her pedaling until her bike was barely rolling fast enough for her to keep it balanced, but no blinding lights appeared in the sky to rescue her. She was just going to have to live through this the same as she'd lived through all the other bad things that had happened to her in the past.

She should have never stopped listening to that little voice inside her head that had kept whispering that it wouldn't last.

Chapter 12

Aunt Joyce was talking on the phone when Birdie went in the house. At first Birdie was glad, because that gave her a chance to get past the kitchen to the bathroom, where she could wash her face before Aunt Joyce saw her. But she couldn't sneak by Kat.

The cat jumped down out of the rocking chair in the living room and walked slowly over to Birdie. It had been obvious for weeks that she was going to have kittens. Now, her tummy low to the floor, Kat rubbed against Birdie's legs and purred.

As Birdie leaned over to quickly stroke the cat before slipping off to the bathroom, Aunt Joyce's voice came out of the kitchen to pierce through her.

"But Barbara, are you sure?" Aunt Joyce was saying with real distress in her voice.

At the sound of her mother's name, Birdie's hand froze on the cat. Birdie had talked to her mother last week. She'd sounded good, cheerful, sober. The treatment was working. Now Birdie stood up and strained hard to hear what Aunt Joyce would say next.

"No, no, that's not it," Aunt Joyce said after a moment's silence. "Birdie's not a bit of trouble, and we love having her here. You know that. I just don't know whether she'll want to stay. She wants to be with you and Kevin.''

Birdie's throat tightened as she listened.

"I can't tell her," Aunt Joyce said finally. "You'll have to do that.''

Birdie couldn't move as the silence came out of the kitchen to wrap around her and whisper all sorts of possibilities in her ear. After a pause, Aunt Joyce went on. "She should be home any time now. She always gets here before dark.''

When Birdie realized her aunt hadn't heard her come in, she backed up to the door, which she opened and slammed shut again. After rubbing her face off on her shirttail, she called out in her brightest voice, "Aunt Joyce, I'm home."

Kat cocked her head first one way and then another as she watched Birdie, but the cat seemed willing to play the scene again as she pushed against Birdie's legs to get her greeting all over.

From the kitchen, Aunt Joyce called back, "Birdie, oh good. Your mother's on the phone. She wants to talk to you.''

Aunt Joyce attempted a smile as she handed Birdie the receiver. Then she bustled out of the kitchen to hover in the hallway.

"Hello," Birdie said into the receiver. She half held her breath as she waited for whatever it was her mother was going to say.

"Good news, Birdie," her mother said. "The doctors say I'm well enough to leave the center.''

"That's good," Birdie said and again waited. Her mother sounded funny, nervous almost.

"It's better than that. It's wonderful.''

"You're over it then? The alcoholism."

"I'll never be over it," her mother said softly. "But the doctors think I can control it now. With a lot of help from my family."

"I've always tried to help you, Mama."

"I know, Birdie. And you've got to help me again now."

"How?" Birdie asked.

"I'm coming to that. Willie's going to come get me here. You know we never did actually get a divorce, and he's willing to give our marriage another try. I think I can make it work this time."

"Kevin will be happy," Birdie said slowly. She felt like she was standing over to the side watching someone else talk to her mother.

"Yes, he needs his father with him." Her mother paused as though hoping Birdie would say something. When she didn't, her mother plunged on. "Anyway, Willie's house is small, only two bedrooms, and he just got this new job. He's not making much money yet, and since you're doing so well there where you are, we thought maybe it'd be better if you just stayed on the rest of this year anyway. You do like your Aunt Joyce and Uncle Albert, don't you? They are nice to you?"

"Yes," Birdie said, a jumble of feelings pushing around inside her. "But who'll take care of Kevin if you get a job?"

"He's in school now, Birdie, and Willie's mother lives close. He's been going over there a lot already."

"Oh," Birdie said.

"I think it's going to work out real well," her mother rushed on. "Mrs. Hansen thinks it's the best idea, too. She says you shouldn't have had to have all the responsibility while I was sick. She says you deserve some time to just be a kid, and since you're getting along so well there on the farm, well, it just seems to be the best thing for everybody.''

Birdie had to make two tries before she could say, ''Yeah, I guess so.''

''I'm so glad you understand, Birdie. You've always been such a good child. I never understood that other social worker that time saying you had problems with those foster families. I knew you wouldn't make problems.''

''I tried not to,'' Birdie said.

Her mother kept talking for a few minutes, but Birdie didn't comprehend much of what she said. She was glad when at last they said good-bye.

When Aunt Joyce heard her hang up the telephone, she came back in the kitchen. She wrung her hands as she said, ''I know it may not be what you want, Birdie, but your uncle and I like having you here with us. We want you to think of the farm as your home as long as you need it.''

''Thank you,'' Birdie said stiffly.

''And I know you and Kevin will be able to visit at vacation times.'' Aunt Joyce couldn't seem to stand it any longer. She came across the room and hugged Birdie as she said, ''It's going to work out all right.''

''Yes,'' Birdie agreed even while inside her head the little voice was reminding her that nothing lasted. She pulled away from Aunt Joyce. ''I think I'll change clothes before supper.''

As soon as she opened the door to the steps that led up to her room, Kat was there in front of her.

Without turning back to look at Aunt Joyce, Birdie said, "I'm not very hungry, Aunt Joyce. Will it be all right if I skip supper tonight?"

"Of course, dear. But in case you change your mind, I'll save you a plate."

Picking up Kat, Birdie carried her up the stairs, where she sat at the desk and stroked the cat while the room grew dark around her. After what seemed like a long time, she turned on her lamp and pulled out her Galiena notebook.

"Galiena didn't know what to do. She'd just found out that the rescue ship that was supposed to pick her up at the end of her mission had broken down and the crew was trying to get it back to Theopolis safely. They couldn't chance picking her up first. No other rescue ship could be sent for months, maybe years.

"Galiena sighed and studied the world around her that she'd learned so much about in recent weeks. The mechanical breakdown of her rescue ship wasn't her only problem. Katura would soon have a family of her own and little time to spend helping Galiena, and her human friend had betrayed her. Sadness began to make Galiena's hair stand on end, for Theopolitans did not let water leak from their eyes when they were sad. That was a custom peculiar to this planet.

"Galiena patted her hair back down and shook away the silly sadness. It would do her no good. She needed to think. Perhaps she could find a way back to Theopolis. She didn't have to wait for another ship. Galiena drew a piece of paper to her to begin drawing her designs for a space-

141

ship big enough to carry one small being and able to travel much faster than the speed of light. Katura lay on the table and purred softly as Galiena worked.''

The next morning Birdie ate her breakfast, even though she still wasn't hungry, because she knew Aunt Joyce wouldn't let her skip two meals in a row without being sure she was sick. At school, Birdie didn't even smile when Howard told her his latest joke. She didn't want to talk to anyone.

As the morning classes crept by, she pretended she was invisible. She didn't even notice when the last of the erasers disappeared under shirts and in purses. She didn't care.

Jobee ran her down after lunch. ''Wait up, Birdie. I've got to talk to you.''

She kept walking, but he grabbed her arm, not seeming to realize that she was invisible.

''What's the matter with you, Birdie? You look sick.''

''The spaceship from Theopolis isn't coming,'' she said.

''Good. I don't want you to go back to Theopolis anyway,'' Jobee said. ''I want to talk to you.''

She made her eyes really focus on him then, and some of her anger from the afternoon before flooded back. She yanked her arm away from him. ''Aren't you afraid Barry will see you?''

''No. I want to apologize for yesterday. I shouldn't have said that about us not being friends. We are friends, Birdie. You're the best friend I've ever had,'' Jobee said seriously. He straightened his glasses and went on. ''I don't want you to be mad at me.''

Birdie tried to go back to being invisible, but she couldn't quite turn on her fade-out signal. Jobee kept staring at her, seeing her. "It's okay, Jobee," she said at last. "I understand."

"I'm not sure I do," Jobee said. "Some of the facts are a little crazy, but I guess everything can't be computed reasonably."

"Barry and the crew will still like you."

"The probabilities of that are slight," Jobee said. "But I don't seem to care that much today." They began walking up the hall together. "Still, I do have an awful feeling that something bad is going to happen today."

"Do the facts point toward it?" Birdie asked.

"I have no facts. This is a feeling." He glanced over at her. "My ability to gather facts and make probability predictions doesn't mean I don't sometimes have feelings."

"So what do you feel is going to happen? Something to do with the erasers?"

"The erasers have all disappeared. Didn't you hear Mr. Wright's announcement at lunch?"

"I guess I wasn't paying attention."

"You haven't acted like you heard anything all morning. But Mr. Wright has more or less put us all under house arrest. They're going to search the lockers and the school today. Whoever is found with erasers is going to be in big trouble. I heard they might even get suspended."

"That doesn't have anything to do with either of us. We don't have any of the erasers."

"Something bad is going to happen." Jobee frowned. "I just know I'm going to get into trouble, and Dad's coming home and he hasn't been home for weeks. I don't know what he'll do if I'm in trouble.''

"But you're not going to be in trouble," Birdie said. "Fact number one, nobody's going to tell that you had anything to do with the eraser heist. Fact number two, the teachers all like you. Fact number three, and the most important one, you don't have the erasers. Right?" She waited for him to nod, then went on. "Stick with your facts, Jobee."

"I hope you're right," Jobee said as they went into math class just before the bell rang.

"I'm always right," Birdie whispered with a smile. The smile lingered even after she'd found her seat. With Jobee still a friend, a few more months here wouldn't be so bad.

A strange feeling hung over the math class as they worked the assignment Mrs. Arnold gave them. Some of the problems were difficult, but Mrs. Arnold calmly told them she couldn't show them how to work any new problems since her board was already crammed full of problems from her former classes.

Out in the hall, they could hear lockers opening and closing as the search began. Birdie hoped Barry had found a good hiding place for the erasers.

By the last class period of the day, the clanging of the lockers in the hall had stopped. Breathing easier, Birdie went into English class, where the students were standing around in bunches. Nobody seemed to be worried about finding a seat as the talking grew louder.

"Where's Mrs. Riggs?" Birdie asked Jana.

Jana shook her head, but Rita, her eyebrows higher

than ever, came running with the answer. "Haven't you heard, Birdie?"

"Heard what?" Birdie asked, hiding her surprise that Rita was talking to her at school.

"They found the erasers. All of them."

Birdie was grabbed by the same feeling that must have been bothering Jobee. "Where?"

"In Jobee's locker. That's why Mrs. Riggs isn't here. She's in the office with him. What do you think they'll do to him?"

"Nothing, because he'll tell them what happened. They won't be able to suspend all of you."

"Riggs won't tell," Barry Wilson said behind Birdie. "He's smarter than that."

Birdie whirled to face him. "You put the erasers in his locker, didn't you?"

"Me?" Barry said with his innocent smile. "You know I wouldn't do that, but since it was mostly his idea, I suppose it's only fair he should get the credit."

"I think it's about time credit is given where credit is due," Birdie said, staring hard at Barry.

"Why not?" Barry laughed. "I'll take credit for the whole plan. It's working like a dream." His smile became a smirk. "But if you're talking about blame, then that goes to the one who gets caught."

"So you won't go to the office and tell Mr. Wright your part in all this." Birdie fixed her eyes on him. When he just laughed at her again, she said, "You know your nose really is funny-looking."

"You're crazy, Honaker. Really crazy," Barry said before he turned his back on her and sauntered away.

"How about the rest of you?" Birdie swept her

145

eyes from one member of the crew to another. "If all of you went to the principal and told him what was going on, he wouldn't suspend you all."

One by one they dropped their eyes.

"Wow, Jobee really knows how to pick friends." Birdie spun away from them and headed toward the door.

Rita grabbed her arm. "Where are you going, Birdie?"

"As far away from Wilson and crew as I can get."

She rushed toward the principal's office, even though she had no idea what she was going to say or do. She just knew she had to do something. Then it came to her. It wasn't a perfect plan. People were still going to get hurt. She thought regretfully for a moment of Aunt Joyce and Uncle Albert, but it was the only way to get Jobee off the hook. Besides, nothing ever lasted for Birdie. She might as well end it herself as wait for someone else to do it for her, and this might just be her spaceship, her way to get back with Kevin and her mother.

With a deep breath, she marched past the secretary at the front desk toward Mr. Wright's office. Jobee and his mother were sitting just outside the door, as though waiting for a verdict to be handed down. Jobee's face was white, and when Mrs. Riggs noticed Birdie there and touched his arm, he jumped.

"What are you doing here, Birdie?" he asked as he pushed his glasses back in place.

"I've come to tell Mr. Wright what really happened."

"He won't believe you," Jobee said.

"Did you tell him?"

"He wouldn't have believed me either."

146

"He'll believe me," Birdie said. Her mouth straightened out thin and tight. "He'll believe me because I'm going to tell him the truth."

"But you don't know what the truth is."

Birdie smiled mysteriously and slipped into the principal's office without saying another word.

Chapter 13

Mr. Wright believed her. Not because she told the truth, but simply because she said what he wanted to hear.

When she finished he said, "You realize this is a very serious matter, Birdie."

"Yes," she said. Now that she'd told him her story, she wished she could just get up and walk away without saying anything else. All those words had exhausted her, and she didn't want to think about what would happen next.

"Why did you put the erasers in Jobee's locker?" Mr. Wright asked.

"I don't know." Birdie shrugged a little.

As Mr. Wright studied her, the look on his face went from stern to puzzled. "I don't understand you, Birdie. I looked over your school records when you transferred here, and frankly, from your high absentee rate at the different schools you've attended, I expected the worst. But you've been doing well here, not only in attendance—your grades are well above average. This was a chance for you to turn yourself around and perform up to your capabilities."

Birdie met his eyes without flinching.

After a minute he went on. "I've known your aunt and uncle a long time. They're good people, and they're trying to help you."

"I know." Birdie dropped her eyes away from his. She thought hard about Jobee's father sitting in the bleachers watching him play ball. She'd done the right thing, the only thing.

There were more questions. Birdie kept her answers vague, but Mr. Wright was satisfied with them.

"I suppose you thought it was funny to cause all this trouble," he said finally.

Birdie stared down at her hands in her lap. "Not really."

"Good. I'm glad you recognize that at least," he said. "You know I'll have to talk to your aunt and uncle."

Birdie, who'd been dreading those words, looked up. "Maybe you could just talk to Miss Franklin. She works for the social services and she's the one who arranged for me to come stay here."

"I'm sure she'll need to be informed, but while you're here, your aunt and uncle are your guardians and thus responsible for your behavior."

"I see." Birdie's mind raced as she tried to think of some way she could soften the blow to her aunt and uncle. "Let me tell them what happened tonight, and then they can come to school with me in the morning to talk to you. Please." Her eyes pleaded with him.

"I guess I can go along with that," Mr. Wright said. "You did come forward on your own, and that fact deserves some consideration." Picking up a pad on his desk, he scribbled something on the top sheet. "Give this to your aunt."

When Birdie left the principal's office at last, Jobee and his mother were gone. Outside the buses were already lined up, so instead of going back to class, Birdie went to her locker. At the first clang of the bell, she was out the door and on the bus. The note the principal had given her burned in her pocket when Uncle Albert smiled at her, but she only smiled back before she found a seat. She still didn't know exactly what she was going to do.

She looked back at the school and thought of Jobee going to basketball practice. She wished she could talk to him about what to do. Together they might be able to brainstorm a solution. Then again, his probabilities were sometimes depressing.

Back at the farm, Birdie simply said "Fine" when Aunt Joyce asked her how school was. The principal's note stayed in her pocket as she ate cookies at the table in the kitchen and watched Aunt Joyce working on a new sweater. The wool in her lap was a soft mixture of brown and cream.

Reluctant to leave the kitchen, Birdie asked, "What are you making?"

"I'm starting a new sweater." Aunt Joyce looked over at Birdie. "For you. I hope you'll like it. It's not a very bright color."

"It looks like Cleopatra."

Aunt Joyce smiled a little. "That's because it's her wool. You can't dye llama wool, you know, but I thought you might think it was fun to have a sweater made of her wool."

Birdie laughed. "You think that will make her quit spitting at me or make her spit at me more?"

"I don't know. You just can't tell about Cleopatra. She's one of a kind."

"Just like your sweaters," Birdie said. "I kept the one you made me when I was a little kid for years. It was the nicest thing I ever owned."

"Why, thank you, Birdie." Aunt Joyce's smile lit up her face. "I hope you'll like this one just as much."

Birdie picked up Kat and, purring, the cat settled in Birdie's lap. Birdie stroked Kat's swollen stomach. "How many kittens do you think Kat is going to have?"

"Several, from the looks of her. We'll have to come up with lots of new names."

"We can't name them until we see them," Birdie said. A strange sadness soaked through Birdie, and she wanted to name them now, sight unseen. After a minute, she asked, "Do you think she'll be a good mother?"

Aunt Joyce stopped clicking her needles for a moment as she answered, "It's hard to say, Birdie, but most cats are fairly good mothers. I'm sure Kat will take good care of her kittens."

"Do you think, I mean now that you know you're going to keep her, that we might change Kat's name?"

"Well, I don't know. What would we call her if we didn't call her Kat?"

"Katura."

"I think that would be fine." Aunt Joyce looked down at her needles again. "Katura seems to fit her. Kat's always been a little plain for such a mysterious cat."

Silence fell over the kitchen then, broken only by the clicking of Aunt Joyce's needles and Katura's purring. Once Birdie thought about breaking that si-

151

lence to tell Aunt Joyce about the note in her pocket. But she didn't know how she would explain it all, and she'd promised not to cause them any trouble. So she stayed silent.

Finally she carefully put Katura back on the floor and stood up. "If it's okay, Aunt Joyce, I'm going to ride down to the sanctuary to see if Mr. Parker needs me to do anything today."

When she got to the nature sanctuary, M.P. was out with a tour. Birdie wandered through the cabin, ran her hand over the map dispenser she and Jobee had made, and then sat down on the ground in the middle of the open space where she had the best view of the trees on all sides of her. The leaves were beginning to fall, and each time Birdie saw the wind shake loose a fresh group of leaves she felt sad. She didn't want to see their beauty come to an end.

When M.P. came back from his tour, they cleaned up around the cabin. As Birdie picked up sticks and trash, she tried to tell him how she felt about the leaves falling.

"The beauty of the trees doesn't end just because the leaves fall." He looked at her with a scowl. "You greenhorn city folks don't understand anything about nature."

"I didn't say I didn't know the leaves had to fall."

"There's all kinds of beauty, girl," M.P. said, his scowl fading and his voice softening. "Leaves aren't all that's pretty. The branches underneath have their own beauty. You can see all sorts of things in the winter that you'd never spot any other time, and when the snow and ice falls, this place turns into a winter wonderland." M.P. turned away from her as though he were suddenly embarrassed by all his words. "But you'll see," he finished shortly.

Later, as Birdie rode her bike home, she tried to picture the trees she passed under without their leaves, but she couldn't. Maybe when winter came, she could look at the trees wherever she was and then imagine what the sanctuary looked like here. Pain swelled up inside her, but she pushed it aside. She shouldn't have let herself like it here so much. Nothing lasted. Nothing. Why hadn't she remembered that?

She pedaled on toward the farm, no longer looking up at the trees.

Then, when she started up the driveway to the farmhouse and saw Jobee's bike leaning against the gate, she didn't feel quite so bad. It had been worth it. No matter what happened next, no matter what her mother did, that wouldn't change the fact that she had a friend. Jobee had sacrificed his chance for popularity at school to be her friend.

He heard her bike on the gravel and came around the house to meet her.

"Hi," she said casually. "What were you doing out back? Visiting with Cleo?"

"As a matter of fact, yes," Jobee said. "I brought an apple for her. I thought perhaps bribery would change her behavior toward me."

"Did it?"

"She ate the apple." Jobee paused for effect before he added, "It gave her more juice to spit at me."

Birdie laughed.

"You should go out and join Cleopatra," Jobee said as he brushed off his sleeve. "She's still laughing, too."

"I'm not sure we'd like Cleo as much if she were nice," Birdie said.

"An interesting theory. I'll have to think about that."

They looked at each other then, and Birdie tried to avoid the question in his eyes. "I've been down to help M.P. clean up a little," she said quickly. She started to tell him about the trees, but Jobee cut her off.

"I know all about the trees. They have bark, leaves, roots, and branches. Tell me what happened at school. What did you tell Mr. Wright?"

"Enough so that you don't have to worry about getting into trouble." Birdie pushed her bike over and propped it against the fence.

"You told him about Barry, and he believed you?"

"He believed what I told him."

"I can't believe it," Jobee said with a sigh of relief. "I was worried that maybe you'd just get into trouble yourself. I didn't think Mr. Wright would believe you."

"Getting him to believe me was no trouble," Birdie said. "He didn't want you to be the culprit anyway."

"But I bet he was surprised when you told him Barry was behind it all. Most of the teachers think Barry's the ideal all-American boy."

"Yeah, I'm sure they do." Birdie looked away from Jobee up toward the sky, where a few stars were glimmering in the deepening darkness.

"What did he say he was going to do?" Jobee asked.

"He didn't say." Birdie didn't want to talk about

the eraser mess anymore. She pointed to the dimmest star overhead and said, "I think that's Theopolis."

"What makes you think so?" Jobee asked as he looked up at the star.

"Instinct. Theopolitans are born with the basic instincts necessary to navigate the skies."

"Actually," Jobee said and adjusted his glasses closer to his head. "Actually all visible stars have already been named. You could probably find out what that particular star is called if you did a little research."

"Just because people here on earth named it something else doesn't mean it's not Theopolis."

"That could be true," Jobee said. "And from the number of stars up there I guess I had better start for home. After Mom's scare today, she's been more aware of whether I'm where I should be or not. English class was a disaster. Everybody was whispering, and Mom was too distracted to do anything about it. I almost wished that she'd get up and start reciting Shakespeare or run down the aisles."

"She'll be back to normal by tomorrow afternoon," Birdie said. "Everything will be."

"I guess we'll just have to wait and see." Jobee got on his bike.

"Good luck in the game tomorrow night," Birdie said as he started off. "Don't forget to square up when you shoot."

"How could I forget?" he called back over his shoulder. "You've told me at least a hundred times."

After supper, Birdie helped with the dishes the same as always. Then she went up to her room and did her homework. She wasn't sure why. She just felt like she should. Only then did she pick up her

Galiena notebook. She read through it, smiling in places. At last, with Katura purring beside her, she wrote a final episode.

"Galiena looked around the farm where she'd spent the last few months. She was going to miss the old couple who had been so nice to her, and she might even miss the monster llama's tricks and laughing eyes. Katura, too, would have to stay behind, as there would soon be baby Katuras.

"The ship from Theopolis had not come, but Galiena had been successful in making another means of transport. However, she couldn't be sure where it would take her. Perhaps if she were lucky, it would run a direct course to Theopolis. More likely it would not, and Galiena would find herself in another strange world with new secrets and dangers.

"She was ready. There was no other way, but still she couldn't keep from regretting leaving this place and the creatures she'd grown fond of. But leave she must. She must try to return to Theopolis and complete her mission.

"Galiena fought against the fear that rose inside her. She was strong. She had powers. She would find a way to complete her mission."

The next morning, Birdie rose before daylight. Quietly she dressed in her most comfortable jeans and shirt, and then, with her canvas bag in her hand, she stood in the middle of the room and looked around. Katura roused herself from her spot on the end of Birdie's bed to come wrap her body in and out around Birdie's legs.

Birdie listened to Katura's purring, and for a moment, she let the good feeling inside her awaken and rumble its purr through her.

After what seemed like a long time, she picked the cat up and put her back on the bed. She rubbed her until Katura was half asleep before she slipped down the stairs and into the kitchen. The nightlight burning in the hall gave Birdie all the light she needed.

Carefully she placed the note on the table. The note said she and Jobee had a project to finish before school that she'd forgotten to tell them about the night before. She hadn't wanted to wake them, and there was no need for them to worry. She'd catch a ride to school with Jobee's mother.

If Aunt Joyce believed what she'd written, Birdie figured she had at least four hours before Mr. Wright called the farm. She had studied the map she'd gotten from the sanctuary the night before, and she thought that would give her enough time to get to the bus station in Louisville.

Birdie felt her pocket for the tenth time since she'd dressed. The money she'd gotten for mowing the yards made a nice, bulky wad under her hand. It would be enough, with some left over for food and emergencies.

Now all that remained to be seen was whether or not her mother would let her stay once she made her way to Willie's house.

As she tiptoed toward the back door, her eyes fell on the bit of sweater in Aunt Joyce's workbasket. A stray piece of yarn had fallen on the floor by the rocking chair. Birdie picked up the yarn and slipped it into her pocket.

Chapter 14

Birdie slowed her bike as she passed the lion-guarded entrance to Jobee's street. In the distance she could just see his house, quiet and solid in the dawning light, and she wondered if his father were home yet. Then she pedaled hard and fast past the street entrance all the way through Brookdale. Only after she left the school behind did she settle into a steady rhythm of pumping. Head down, she concentrated on moving her feet on the pedals as if she were in a long-distance race.

She kept on the smaller roads. As the cars and trucks whizzed past her, she pretended she was only a whisper of wind passing the houses and stores. No one would see her, and she saw no one.

After she'd been riding a long time, she pulled her bike off the road into a thicket of trees to study her map. Panic jumped up inside her as she looked first at the road she'd just left, then at the flat blue mark on the highway map. She couldn't be sure they were the same. There were no road signs, no clue as to where she was. Perhaps she'd made a wrong turn. Maybe more than one.

Discouraged, Birdie sat down on the ground instead of heading back toward the road. Even if she knew for sure she wasn't lost, she didn't know lots of other things, such as what her mother would do when Birdie got to Willie's house. Kevin would want her to stay even if he didn't need her as much as he once had. Still, if it came to a choice, Kevin would choose Willie. If Birdie had a father, she might choose the same.

Avery Honaker. Had there ever been such a man? Perhaps the wild story she'd told Jobee was true. Perhaps her father had been an alien.

Birdie looked at the sky, but the sun was shining brightly. All the stars had faded from sight hours ago. Back at the farm Cleopatra and the sheep would be moving about the pasture, clipping off the grass close to the ground. Reever would be sprawled on the porch, his long ears flopped out on each side of him. Katura would be sleeping in the rocking chair, and Aunt Joyce would be knitting the brown and cream llama wool into a sweater. Maybe she would finish it anyway and send it to Birdie.

Birdie looked back at the road. With a sigh, she stood up and pushed her bike back toward the road. For a second as she mounted the bicycle, she wanted to turn back the way she'd come, retrace her route, and be at the farm.

Nothing lasted, she reminded herself as she started pedaling in the other direction. The good feeling she'd had at the farm couldn't have lasted either. She'd had her two months.

She was on the right road. A half hour later she saw a sign, and then another half hour got her to the outskirts of the city. She had to ask four times for directions to the bus station, but finally she turned down the right street. She leaned her bike against the side of the building and went inside.

Birdie hardly noticed the people milling about as she headed straight for the ticket counter. Then somebody stepped in front of her and blocked her way. Birdie's eyes flew open wide as she said, "Jobee!"

It couldn't be him. She was imagining it. All this pretending to be Galiena must have given Birdie some of her alien powers, and seeing Jobee in front of her was only some kind of mind trick. She reached out her hand, half expecting it to go through her vision of him, but her hand felt the smooth cloth of his jacket.

Still, he hadn't said anything. He just kept staring at her, the blue of his eyes dark behind his glasses.

"What are you doing here?" Birdie asked. If he didn't answer her, he might still be a vision in spite of the true bulk of him there in front of her.

"I'm not running away." His voice was hard and angry to match his eyes.

"Neither am I," Birdie said softly. "I'm just going home."

"I thought you said the spaceship from Theopolis wasn't coming."

"Not that home. I'm going back to Chicago. My mother called. She's out of the hospital now."

"I know," Jobee said.

"Then what are you doing here? Why aren't you at school? What about your father coming to see you play ball?"

"You want facts or feelings?" Jobee asked.

"Facts."

"Fact one, I'm here because I knew you'd be here.

Fact two, I'm not at school because I'm here. Fact three, my father is here with me. He brought me."

"That explains everything," Birdie said as she looked around for someone she thought might be Jobee's father.

"Dad's watching the other entrance. I told him what you looked like. But I don't think what I said explains anything. You're the one who needs to explain things."

"I told you. I'm going to my mother's."

"That's what you said, but sometimes you don't tell the factual truth. I know some of that truth. I know your mother wants you to stay at the farm. I know you didn't tell your aunt and uncle you were leaving. I know you lied to Mr. Wright about the erasers."

"You know a lot. I guess that's how you knew where to find me."

"The probabilities of that were easy to figure out. My mother called Mr. Wright last night and found out what you told him. I went to your house this morning to talk to you about it, but you were gone, supposedly to my house, which I knew wasn't true. I knew how much money you had from your mowing jobs. Remember, you told me last week. Not enough for a plane ticket. I saw the road map in your pocket when you came home from the sanctuary last night. So the probability was that you'd end up here if you didn't get lost or run over or kidnapped on the way. Since there was nothing I could do about those possibilities, my father and I came here to wait."

"I guess I left too many clues," Birdie said. She

161

hesitated and then asked, "Was Aunt Joyce very upset?"

"Yes."

"Oh." Birdie looked down at the floor. She felt a little sick inside thinking about Aunt Joyce. "I guess she called Miss Franklin."

"I don't know anything about a Miss Franklin."

"I wish I didn't," Birdie said. She thought about Miss Franklin talking to Mr. Wright and Aunt Joyce. Lying and running away would be worse than skipping school. She wondered where they might send her next, and she wished she hadn't left Jobee so many clues. She looked up at him. "You could pretend you didn't see me, Jobee."

"You mean tell lies like you've been doing."

"I didn't lie to you, Jobee, only to Mr. Wright."

"That's the only part I haven't been able to exactly figure out. Why did you tell Mr. Wright that you put the erasers in my locker? I can't believe you were protecting Barry."

"No. It was the only way to keep you out of trouble."

"Did you think I'd feel better knowing you were in trouble instead?"

"I didn't think you would worry that much about it. I mean, I know we're friends. But I'd be gone, and you'd get to play in the ball game tonight. I know how much that meant to you, since your father was going to be here and everything."

"It didn't mean that much." Jobee looked at her a few seconds before he went on. "I deserved to take some of the blame for the erasers. A lot of it was my idea. I didn't want you to go away."

"Fact or feeling?" Birdie asked softly.

"Both," Jobee said matter-of-factly. Then he took hold of Birdie's hand. "Let's go find my father."

"Then what?" Birdie asked as they began threading their way through the people waiting for buses.

"Then we go home, and you tell everybody the truth for a change. Unless." He stopped and looked back at her. "Unless you really don't want to go back to Brookdale. Then I guess I could say I hadn't seen you."

Birdie hesitated, then shook her head. "No, you're right. I shouldn't have run away. I need to tell Aunt Joyce and Uncle Albert I'm sorry, no matter what else happens." The thought of facing her aunt and uncle made her stomach lurch. Not only that, but she'd have to answer to Miss Franklin, who would read through her file and decide Birdie's fate.

Birdie wouldn't worry about that now. Instead she'd think about seeing the farm again, and Katura and even Cleopatra. At the thought, the warm feeling stretched a little inside her. It didn't actually purr, but it was still there.

After they found Jobee's father, he smiled at her with Jobee's smile and didn't say a word about her running away. He just loaded her bicycle into the trunk of his car, bought them all something to eat, and then talked about the faces at the bus station. Before they got back to Brookdale he was considering the feasibility of a story on those faces and their destinations.

While he and Jobee talked easily about the likely backgrounds of the people they'd seen, Birdie sat between them and thought about what she would say to Aunt Joyce and Uncle Albert. She'd called them from the station to tell them she was all right. The sound of tears had mingled with relief and questions in Aunt Joyce's voice.

The closer they came to Brookdale, the more nervous Birdie became, until finally she had to sit on her hands to keep them from shaking. As they passed the school, Birdie told Jobee he should stop. "If you go part of the day, they might still let you play tonight." She glanced over at his father. "When you're absent, you can't play."

Mr. Riggs smiled at her. "I don't think Jobee's too worried about the ball game tonight."

"But you came all the way from Mexico to see him play." Birdie looked down.

"That's not so far," Jobee's father said. "A few hours on an airplane. Besides, Jobee tells me the possibility of him getting to play is slight." Jobee's father looked over at her and winked. "You know Jobee and his probabilities. He's usually right. And if there was ever any choice, I'd much rather watch him helping a friend than pitching a basketball at a hoop."

Birdie had to blink hard to keep back the tears. "I'm sorry I messed everything up."

Jobee poked her leg. "Don't be silly, Birdie. Dad's staying a few days. Maybe I'll get into the next game. The probability should be improved by a few more practice sessions."

As Birdie had expected, Miss Franklin's car was pulled up in front of the house when they got back to the farm, but Aunt Joyce hadn't been the one who called her. Instead Mr. Wright had contacted her when Birdie didn't show up with her aunt and uncle for their appointed meeting.

By then Jobee had told the principal the truth about

164

the erasers in his locker. Rita and a couple of other kids Birdie barely knew backed up his story.

Miss Franklin told her about it when she asked to talk to Birdie alone. Birdie watched her and waited, glad that Katura had stayed curled up beside her on the couch. With the tips of her fingers, Birdie touched Katura's head so softly it didn't disturb the cat's nap as Miss Franklin stared at the file folder in her lap. Birdie could tell she wasn't reading it. Her eyes stayed fixed on the same spot too long.

"You shouldn't have lied to Mr. Wright," Miss Franklin said at last. She raised her eyes to look at Birdie.

"I thought it would help Jobee," Birdie said quietly.

"I know, but you should have thought about the consequences of your actions. How it would make your aunt and uncle feel."

"I did. That's why I left."

"Oh, Birdie," Miss Franklin said. "Running away never solves anything."

Birdie just looked at her without saying anything. She'd already said she was sorry and that she knew it was the wrong thing to do. Birdie had resigned herself to whatever they decided to do with her next. So now she waited.

After a minute, Miss Franklin sighed. "I suppose I should inform Mrs. Hansen. See what she thinks."

"You haven't told Mrs. Hansen?" The first bit of hope edged into Birdie's heart.

"Not yet. She's such a stickler for doing everything a certain pre-set way, and sometimes people and especially children don't fit in her slots so well." Miss Franklin seemed to realize what she'd said and

165

hurried on. "I don't mean that she hasn't got the best interests of everyone in mind. She just sees things a bit differently than we do out here."

Again there was silence. Again Birdie waited, but now inside her the warm feeling was raising its head, watching warily to see if it might be able to stay.

"Your aunt and uncle want you to stay," Miss Franklin went on. "They want you to think of this as your home, even though they understand that you might rather be with your mother."

"My mother doesn't want me," Birdie said.

Miss Franklin's eyes softened. "It's not exactly that she doesn't want you, Birdie. It's just that she needs more time to adjust to everything. And you need more time to be able to be a young girl. Would you like to stay here?"

Birdie met her eyes and said, "Yes, please." And then there were tears tumbling out of her eyes even as the happy feeling inside her began to purr. She'd found a place to belong for as long as she needed it. Katura stood up and rubbed against her arm.

Miss Franklin ignored Birdie's tears as she shuffled her papers and shoved them back in the folder. "Then that's settled. I expect to hear only good things from you in the coming months, Birdie."

Several days later, Jobee and Birdie slowly rode their bikes toward home after working a late tour at the sanctuary. Occasionally a leaf drifted down in front of them to join the layer already on the road, and here and there, Birdie spotted a tree with the beauty of its limbs already exposed to her eyes. Things were almost back to the way they were before the erasers had been found in Jobee's locker.

166

At school, no one had been suspended. Instead they'd had to work off their punishment by cleaning blackboards, picking up trash, and scrubbing every trace of graffiti off any surface in the school.

Barry still had his crew, but he'd lost some of his power over the rest of the kids and all of his power over Jobee. A new group was forming in the halls and at lunchtime. In this group, it not only didn't matter if you were a little different, it was better.

Now, as Birdie rode along beside Jobee, she still felt the soreness in her legs from her long bicycle ride away from Brookdale. She looked over at Jobee and said, "I'm glad your father got to see a ball game before he had to go back to Mexico."

"I'm not sure that was too thrilling," Jobee said.

"You got to play."

"Two minutes, fourteen seconds. Two points, one foul, one turnover, no steals, no rebounds. Not exactly impressive."

"You'll be more impressive next time," Birdie said as they eased to a stop at the end of the drive leading up to the farmhouse. Inside her the purr was rumbling loudly. She still missed Kevin, but it was good to belong somewhere without having to actually earn it. To just belong because somebody wanted you to.

"The probabilities of me ever being an impressive ball player are slim to none," Jobee said. "However, perhaps I will be impressive at other things. Maybe an inventor." He looked up at the sky, where the first stars were appearing.

"What about me?" Birdie asked, looking up, too.

167

"What do you think the probabilities are that I'll ever do anything impressive?"

"Very high, I'd say. You may be a great science fiction writer." Birdie had let him read her Galiena story the day before. Jobee went on, his eyes still on the sky. "Or perhaps you'll just be a great scientist."

"Time will tell, I suppose," Birdie said. "What are you looking at?"

He pointed toward a star. "That's the star you said was Theopolis. Someday we'll build our spaceship, Birdie, and go there."

"What will we do when we get there?" Birdie asked.

"What do you think? We'll find your father, and we'll thank him for once upon a time being an alien spy."

Birdie stared at the star a long time before she said, "Do you think my father might really be there?"

"I couldn't say for sure. The probabilities of such things are impossible to figure. But sometimes feelings matter more than facts."

Birdie watched Jobee ride away before she rode on toward the farmhouse, where the light streaming off the porch had been left on for her. After supper, Birdie would start a new adventure. This one would be about an earth girl and boy making their way into deep space. The monsters Galiena had faced would pale compared to the unknown monsters that might await Avery and Joseph in the farthest reaches of the universe. Perhaps Jobee was right. Perhaps the earth girl might even find her father.

Birdie smiled as she ran up the porch steps and into the house. Katura didn't come to meet her. She'd had her kittens the day before, and now Aunt Joyce and Birdie were considering names.

"I'm home, Aunt Joyce," Birdie called as she took off the sweater made from Cleo's wool and hurried toward the kitchen. Inside her the good feeling purred, and it was a feeling that Birdie knew would last.

Celebrating 40 Years of Cleary Kids!

CAMELOT presents
CLEARY FAVORITES!

☐ **HENRY HUGGINS**
70912-0 ($3.50 US/$4.25 Can)

☐ **HENRY AND BEEZUS**
70914-7 ($3.50 US/$4.25 Can)

☐ **HENRY AND THE
CLUBHOUSE**
70915-5 ($3.50 US/$4.25 Can)

☐ **ELLEN TEBBITS**
70913-9 ($3.50 US/$4.25 Can)

☐ **HENRY AND RIBSY**
70917-1 ($3.50 US/$4.25 Can)

☐ **BEEZUS AND RAMONA**
70918-X ($3.50 US/$4.25 Can)

☐ **RAMONA AND HER FATHER**
70916-3 ($3.50 US/$4.25 Can)

☐ **MITCH AND AMY**
70925-2 ($3.50 US/$4.25 Can)

☐ **RUNAWAY RALPH**
70953-8 ($3.50 US/$4.25 Can)

☐ **HENRY AND THE
PAPER ROUTE**
70921-X ($3.50 US/$4.25 Can)

☐ **RAMONA AND HER MOTHER**
70952-X ($3.50 US/$4.25 Can)

☐ **OTIS SPOFFORD**
70919-8 ($3.50 US/$4.25 Can)

☐ **THE MOUSE AND THE
MOTORCYCLE**
70924-4 ($3.50 US/$4.25 Can)

☐ **SOCKS**
70926-0 ($3.50 US/$4.25 Can)

☐ **EMILY'S RUNAWAY
IMAGINATION**
70923-6 ($3.50 US/$4.25 Can)

☐ **MUGGIE MAGGIE**
71087-0 ($3.50 US/$4.25 Can)

Stories of Adventure From
THEODORE TAYLOR
Bestselling Author of

TEETONCEY
71024-2/$3.50 US/$4.25 Can

Ben O'Neal searched the darkened shore for survivors from the ship wrecked by the angry surf. He spotted the body on the sand—a girl of about ten or eleven; almost his own age—half drowned, more dead than alive. The tiny stranger he named Teetoncey would change everything about the way Ben felt about himself.

TEETONCEY AND BEN O'NEAL
71025-0/$3.50 US/$4.25 Can

Teetoncey, the little girl Ben O'Neal rescued from the sea after the shipwreck of the *Malta Empress*, had not spoken a word in the month she had lived with Ben and his mother. But then the silence ends and Teetoncey reveals a secret about herself and the *Malta Empress* that will change all their lives forever.

THE ODYSSEY OF BEN O'NEAL
71026-9/$3.50 US/$4.25 Can

At thirteen, Ben O'Neal is about to begin his lifelong dream—to go to sea. But before Ben sails, he receives an urgent message from Teetoncey, saying she's in trouble. And somehow Ben knows that means trouble for him.